LAWLESS

STEEL DEMONS MC BOOK ONE

CRYSTAL ASH

SDMC series playlist

All American Nightmare - Hinder
Notorious - Adelitas Way
Hail to the King - Avenged Sevenfold
Joan of Arc - In This Moment
Radioactive - Imagine Dragons
Bad Company - Five Finger Death Punch
Love Me to Death - No Resolve
(Don't Fear) The Reaper - HIM
David - Noah Gunderson
Machine Gun Blues - Social Distortion
Wanted Dead or Alive - Chris Daughtry
I Get Off - Halestorm
You Shook Me All Night Long - AC/DC
Nobody Praying for Me - Seether
Loyal to No One - Dropkick Murpheys
Be Free - King Dude & Chelsea Wolfe
Raise Hell - Dorothy

Click here to listen on Spotify!

Prologue

MARIPOSA

Have you ever been to a graduation that felt like a funeral?

That was exactly how mine felt. Somber. Tense. Everyone, graduates and faculty alike, kept their true feelings under a neutral mask. No one wanted to say it, but we all knew.

Instead of celebrating our bright new future, we were already mourning the death of it.

The Collapse happened during my freshman year at Northwestern Medical College. We were still bright-eyed and hopeful then, so confident we'd be the ones to restore order and justice to the world upon graduation.

The United States of America ceased to exist and every state became its own independent faction with its own laws and regulations. Some slid right back into the dark ages, stripping away the rights of women and minorities as their people cheered.

Others went in the complete opposite direction, welcoming *all* people and practices with open arms.

This led to violent internal conflicts as ideas and opinions clashed.

Still, we remained hopeful.

Then the wars broke out, too many to count or name. Some dragged on for years, others mere skirmishes that lasted less than a day.

Every morning, news spread of another self-appointed governor being assassinated, or the invasion of one territory into another. Borders were redrawn and new capitals erected, always by some power-hungry maniac who seized the opportunity when it suited him best. Until the next one assassinated him and started the process all over again.

Those who weren't killed or kidnapped, and could afford to do so, fled the country. Many took the dangerous trek to Canada, others fled to Latin America, although the situation wasn't much better down there. And the ultra-rich, the ones who could still afford plane passage after half of the international airports were bombed, flew across the oceans to greener pastures in Europe and Africa.

Most African countries succeeded in overthrowing their tyrannical dictators in the last century. America had apparently forgotten how to do it. The home of the brave became a land of lawlessness.

And we, the graduating class of 2100, would be the ones inheriting that land.

Congratulations to us.

So, can you blame us for having such a grim graduation ceremony? Not even anyone's parents cracked a smile.

Dr. Brooks, the dean of the Gonzalez Nursing School, stepped up to the podium like he was about to deliver a eulogy.

"I prepared a speech for today that was full of hope and optimism," he began, his jaw tense as he took in the faces of the graduates. "But then I heard the news this morning and realized what a disservice it would be to the young people at this ceremony if I were to sugarcoat the truth."

Aside from paper programs and graduation robes fluttering in the warm breeze, no one made a sound. Early this morning, the battle that had been waging for weeks sixty miles south of here, had ceased. Because the last of those defending our last little shred of independence had been gunned down by armed rebels. As of nine o'clock this morning, Warsaw County, Texas had been annexed into the Republic of Texahoma.

Dr. Brooks looked out grimly over all of the graduates, as if he were sentencing us to death himself.

"The world you have inherited is cruel," he said. "It's unjust. It's lawless and unfair. Your generation will be the one to pay for our shortcomings. Our sorrys are too little, too late."

In the silence between his words, the wind carried sounds of gunfire, explosions, and screams from the distant battleground. Although at this point, it was nothing more than a massacre.

No one reacted. We had all gotten used to those sounds.

The faculty in attendance wore harrowed expressions throughout the speech, their eyes staring blankly forward. It was clear that no one disagreed with him.

"There is only one piece of advice I can give to you all," his voice cracked as he went on. "Be better than what we've become. Bring compassion and heart back to this violent world."

———

"YOU'VE GOTTA BE KIDDING ME."

I rolled my eyes toward the clock on the wall. It had been nearly an hour since I was put on hold and the looping music made me want to blow my brains out.

And get lost in all the other brain matter scattered across the street? I don't think so, sister.

"Sorry to keep you waiting. What can I do for you?"

Finally.

"Yeah, hi. I'm trying to get my nursing license registered."

A pause stretched on for just a few moments too long.

"What's your name?"

"Mariposa Wilder."

Another pause.

"I'm sorry. I can't. There's nothing I can do."

"What?" I pulled the phone back from my ear and looked at it like something wasn't working. "What do you mean? I graduated from Northwestern Medical College this morning. I *need* this license to be able to work." Why I had to explain this to someone whose job it was to process licenses was beyond me.

"I'm sorry," the person on the other line repeated, their voice cracking with emotion. "I can't. They'll shoot me if I do."

My heart squeezed in my chest like a cruel fist had wrapped around it.

"They've already gotten to the capital?" I squeaked, my voice lost in disbelief.

"They decreed it not even a half hour ago," the voice answered, seconds away from sobbing. "In the Republic of Texahoma, women are forbidden from holding any kind of medical license."

ONE

MARIPOSA

THREE YEARS LATER

The van lurched to a stop. I grabbed my pack like it would slip away from me before sliding my arms through the straps. The driver's eyes in the rearview mirror told me enough. He wouldn't be driving any further west.

I waited for the half dozen other people hitching a ride to get off before rising from the back seat. As I approached him, I pulled a small baggie from my pocket and held it out to him.

"For your trouble," I muttered.

He just scowled as he snatched the single tablet of valium from me. "You're a fool to come out this far west. The biker gangs eat girls like you alive."

"I'll survive." Those words have been a mantra I've repeated for years. So far, it proved to be true so I wasn't about to doubt it yet.

"After they get their hands on ya," he shook his head, "you might be wishin' for death." With that, he shooed me off his vehicle and drove off in a cloud of dust and exhaust.

I took a moment to observe my surroundings. The first thing I noticed was the fucking heat. This used to be Phoenix, Arizona. Now, like everywhere else, its name and borders changed depending on who was in charge. The latest I heard it being referred to was Old Phoenix.

Creative, these tyrants.

Miles of dry, dusty desert surrounded me in all directions, with the occasional saguaro cactus standing tall like soldiers. A mountain range stood off in the distance, the only not-flat part of the landscape. It would have been pretty and majestic, if anybody could bring themselves to feel good about anything these days.

The van driver dropped his passengers off in front of a service station, which had once been a hotel. Now, these places provided everything from temporary shelter, food, cheap hookers referred to as service girls, and if they were lucky, medical services. Which was what I hoped to provide.

Gripping the edges of my bag straps, I headed for the building that had seen better days. Weeds grew tall, choking off the once charming landscaping. Dust and mud caked the exterior walls and the glass front door, which was also scarred with a few bullet holes.

But I had to count my blessings. There were no motorcycles parked outside. At least not yet.

The smell of must greeted me as I stepped inside. No one bothered to clean anymore, not when gangs and deviants tore through homes and places like these to ransack goods. Even in the twenty-second century, humans still got the urge to pillage and loot.

With the lobby completely empty, I bypassed the front desk and headed straight for the kitchen. Not that I was hoping to run into a biker gang, but the quietness of this place unnerved me. People usually flocked to places like this once their homes were no longer theirs.

Crossing the dining area, I pushed open a swinging door to find a remarkably clean, stainless steel kitchen. And three people cooking.

"Hello," the girl of about sixteen greeted me first while the two adults watched me with suspicious eyes.

"Hi," I said. "Um, I'm a nur—a medic. Are you in need of medical services at this station?" *Please say yes.*

Even after three years of being strictly forbidden to call myself a nurse, it was still a habit.

The man, balding with curly grey hair, wiped his hands on his apron, still looking at me warily.

"You got supplies?" he asked.

I nodded sharply. "Pain medication, a wide range of antibiotics and antivirals, sterile tools for minor surgeries, general first aid gear. I also have some pregnancy tests and different forms of birth control."

His eyebrows shot up at that. In a place full of prostitutes and limited amounts of food, no one wanted extra mouths to feed.

"What'll ya have in return?" he asked.

Since the US Dollar became essentially worthless during the Collapse, bartering became the main currency. Some factions tried establishing their own but they then ran into the problem of no other territory accepting that currency.

"Room and board for roughly two weeks," I said. "And food." My eyes fell to their cutting boards, where potatoes, onions, and carrots sat waiting to finish being chopped.

The older woman spoke up next, her bun unable to contain her wild, frizzy grey hair.

"Can you cook and serve up some food to guests?" *Or are you too good for that?* I heard the hidden question in her voice loud and clear.

"I can do basic cooking and yes, I'll do whatever other tasks you would like. Cleaning and such, too." *But I won't sell my body.*

The couple exchanged a look and a quick nod before the man addressed me.

"We have a deal. But you stay no more than two weeks."

"That's fine," I nodded eagerly, ready for even a dirty, bug-infested bed over sleeping on rest stop benches.

"Gretchen will show you to your room, where you can drop your things." The man picked up his knife and resumed his potato chopping. "Then you come straight back here and help us prepare for tonight."

"What's tonight?" I asked, suddenly aware of the piles and piles of food strewn across the steel counter. It looked as though a large group of people were about to eat like kings.

"The Steel Demons MC will be riding through and

staying," the man answered, steadfast in his chopping. "They have massive appetites, and not just for food."

————

THE TEENAGE GIRL, Gretchen, informed me all about the Steel Demons while we chopped through an endless sea of potatoes, carrots, and celery.

"They ride through here twice a month," she told me. "Reaper, their president, worked out some kind of deal with the owners, Tom and Liza. The whole club stops here on the way to their destination and on the way back. Their club house is way up in Old Flagstaff somewhere. The Doomsdayers say that place is the mouth of Hell itself. Nothing but sin and violence."

I absorbed her words as my stainless blade went *chop-chop-chop* through the vegetables.

"Why is their president called Reaper?" I asked.

"Because," Gretchen lowered her voice, despite the two of us being the only ones in the kitchen, "seeing his club is a death omen. The minute you hear their bikes in the distance, someone's time is up."

"So the rumors are true." I heard whispers of the notorious biker gang all the way in East Texas. One of my patients, a guy hopped up on painkillers from a broken arm, swore they were actual demons, complete with a pack of hellhounds running alongside their bikes.

Gretchen nodded. "The Steel Demons control the southwestern desert from the San Diego Gulf to the Sandia Mountains, and they didn't do that by asking nicely. Wherever they go, hell follows."

She put on a bright smile, her demeanor changing from spooky story teller back to bubbly sixteen-year-old. "They're not so bad when they stop here, though. We're one of the few service centers that still have cured meat and cheese, and they pay well for it."

"They've never hurt you?" I was genuinely surprised. "Or your parents?"

"Oh, Tom and Liza aren't my parents. They just took me in after I was dumped here on their doorstep. And no. The club pretty much eats our food, drinks our ale, stays a few nights to rest, and then they leave. Sure, they're messy and sometimes they fight and break stuff, which is annoying. And it sounds like they're rough with the service girls sometimes, but no one has died since I've been here."

Oh. Well, at least there's that.

"How long have you been here?" I dumped two handfuls of chopped potatoes into a bowl, then emptied the bowl into the awaiting pot of boiling water on the stove.

"About three months." Gretchen hacked off the end of a carrot and brought it to her mouth, biting down with a loud crunch.

"And how's that been? Okay?" I helped myself to a carrot snack as well.

She chewed thoughtfully before answering. "I'm still alive. That's the best you can hope for in a world like this, right?"

With so many dying senselessly in the skirmishes over territory, and plenty more dying from treatable conditions due to the lack of medical care, I felt inclined to agree with her.

But I could still remember a time when people wanted so much more out of life. They wanted stable jobs, degrees from universities, families and friends who loved them, maybe even the occasional luxury like a vacation or a pet.

Then the Collapse happened and the world turned to shit. Humanity couldn't afford to focus on luxury and comfort if we wanted to survive. Mild-mannered family men, like my father, turned into ruthless killers out of necessity. Mom and I cried daily for months when Dad came home from the border skirmishes drenched in blood.

I wondered if the Steel Demons had always been fearsome bikers or if they had been normal citizens at one point, too. The Collapse seemed to bring out the worst in everyone. Self-preservation became the only goal at the forefront of everyone's mind, which ironically, only led to more widespread suffering.

For those that preyed on the weak and sought control in the most sadistic ways, the Collapse was an answered prayer. I heard horror stories of women being treated like cattle, rounded up in corrals and used for breeding. Others said slavery had returned in the territories that was once the South. No one could verify what was true or not, but those whispers made me grateful that being forbidden from receiving my nursing license was the worst that happened in East Texas.

"What brought you out this way?" Gretchen asked,

dumping her bowl of chopped carrots into a separate pot of boiling water.

"I was hoping to find women's groups out west, or just a place I could be a medic without the risk of going to jail," I told her. "I got my nursing degree the same day East Texas got annexed. Women were outlawed from holding any kind of medical license within hours of me graduating."

"At least you got a degree," Gretchen mumbled. "I was pulled out of school at fourteen and sent to a girls' camp. They said we didn't need to know how to read, write, or do math. Being a good, Godly wife was all that mattered and that's what they would teach us."

"Ugh." I shook my head, still disgusted by this jarring, new reality although I was no longer surprised. Girls' camps were popping up all over the place, turning girls and young women into docile, obedient wives for men to purchase.

"How did you get out of there?" I put down my knife and stretched out my hand, my fingers cramping up from all the chopping.

She gave a sly smirk. "My ex-husband bought me, but pushed me out of a moving car right in front of this place when I almost bit his dick off."

"Holy shit! On the highway? It's amazing that you survived!"

"I knew to roll," she shrugged. "Just got a bit of road rash and a sprained wrist. And I've been here ever since."

I considered asking her if she wanted to go with me after I left in two weeks. We could keep heading north toward Canada. Women's rights groups were supposedly all along the border, taking in refugees. Gretchen could finish her education and with luck, I might be able to call myself a nurse again.

But I held my tongue and kept chopping. I just met this girl and wasn't sure if I wanted a travel companion for the next few thousand miles. The loneliness sucked, but it was better than waking up to having half of my supplies stolen. Lesson learned—I could only trust myself in this lawless world.

After a few moments of chopping and cooking, a sound like continuous thunder drowned out everything else. My stomach flipped over on itself, knowing it could only be a crew of motorcycles descending on the inn like a pack of wild dogs coming in for the kill.

"They're here!" Gretchen wiped her hands on her apron and ran to the large walk-in refrigerator. She returned holding two frosted glass pitchers. "Help me fill these up with ale? They like it cold and ready to drink first thing when they arrive."

I took one and followed her to the kegerator, noticing the tremor in her hand as she pulled the tap handle to let the beer flow. For as non-murderous as the Steel Demons were to this place, they apparently still scared the shit out of her.

And if she really did nearly bite the dick off the abusive man who owned her, seeing her tremble at the sound of growling bikes made me especially uneasy.

The Texas and Texahoma territories had their fair share of biker gangs, too, but none had a reputation as notorious as the Steel Demons. As I filled up my pitcher and followed Gretchen out to the lobby, I wondered if not dying by their hands was really the better option.

The front doors burst open with a bang just as we set the pitchers on the coffee tables in front of the couches. Raucous laughter followed booted footsteps as six tall, leather-clad figures entered the lobby, their mere presence commanding respect and fear.

The man leading them leveled his gaze at me. Gretchen and I had dropped off the pitchers and were scurrying back to the kitchen for more, but those catlike green eyes seemed to nail my feet to the floor.

Dark brown hair fell across his forehead as if tousled by a helmet. A straight nose sat above full lips that scowled cruelly at me. Dark stubble peppered an angular jaw and olive, sun-kissed skin.

It stunned me how handsome and young he was. Bikers didn't look like *this*. They were old and grizzled with long hair and beards. Like scary, monstrous versions of Santa Claus.

With the way this man looked at me, though, I had no doubt he was capable of monstrous things.

My eyes fell to his leather cut, where the word PRESIDENT was embroidered on the left side. A curving scythe patch hung ominously over the word, leaving no question as to who this man was.

Reaper. The man who rode with the wrath of Hell at his back.

A growling sound brought my eyes lower, to the massive Doberman Pinscher at his side. I'd never seen such a huge dog, nor one that looked so ready to rip out my throat with a single command from its owner. The dog's black coat had a glossy, healthy sheen, but nothing shone as brightly as those white teeth it bared at me.

"Come, Hades." Reaper's voice was softer than I imagined for someone with such a reputation behind him.

I blinked like a spell had been broken as Reaper's eyes shifted away from me, heading toward the furthest couch with a beer pitcher in front of it. Hades trotted obediently at his side.

His men filed in after him, throwing their booted feet on the coffee tables as they drank directly from the pitchers. Some drank half the containers in a single gulp. No wonder we needed so many.

Reaper wasn't the only one with a pet. A man with a falcon on his shoulder sat at the second couch. He had golden hair falling down to his shoulders in soft waves. Women used to kill for hair like that, when looking nice was once important to us.

His eyes were blue as a bright summer sky and his mouth formed a wide smile, the complete opposite of Reaper's hard scowl. The blonde man caught my eye as he raised a pitcher to his mouth and winked at me over the rim.

Shit, I forgot there were service girls here. Now these men probably thought I was one.

I turned on my heel and headed back to the kitchen, where Gretchen had two more full pitchers waiting and was in the middle of filling a third. Taking a deep breath to steel myself before going back out there, I wrapped my fingers around the handles and let the breath out.

It didn't matter what these men looked like. They

were murderers, thieves, and probably rapists. They reached their godlike level of fame with violence and brutality. I couldn't let my guard down for a single minute.

I was a mouse in a pit of snakes, and I *had* to survive.

TWO

REAPER

Not even the service girl crawling into my lap could distract me from the new kitchen server. With hazel eyes intent and focused, red lips tight, and rich brown hair cascaded down her back in a loose ponytail, she served food and drinks to my club along with the blonde teenager we'd seen here before.

"I missed you," a raspy voice whispered in my ear while a pair of stretchmarked, used-up tits shoved themselves into my face. "The way you fucked me last time, mmm! It was all I could think about."

"Look, can I get a minute to breathe?" I leaned away from the whore rubbing on me like a cat in heat. I couldn't remember this one's name, but she was blocking my view from the pretty little new girl.

"Sure, honey. Just let me know when you want me." She gave me a wink and squeezed my dick through my pants before rising up to offer her services to my men. Sure enough, she hopped on Brick's cock right when he was in the middle of a conversation with Big G.

The sound of over-exaggerated moans and slapping flesh faded in the background as I popped a fat cheese cube in my mouth. I washed it down with the last of the ale on the table, hoping the new girl would hurry her ass out to refill it.

Jandro took a seat next to me, leaning back on the couch with a sigh. "I cannot fucking wait to sleep in an actual bed tonight. Think I'll grab two girls while I'm at it."

"How are the steeds?" I asked.

"Fine. Just had to clear a bunch of dust from Shadow's bike. Yours is getting low on oil, but should be fine until we make it back to Sheol."

My vice president was not only my second in command, but the most accomplished motorcycle mechanic I'd ever seen. He'd know exactly what was wrong with someone's ride just from the sound she made.

"Damn," Jandro breathed softly, looking across the lounge to the kitchen. The door had been propped open with how much running the girls had to go back and forth.

I followed his gaze to the new girl, fast on her feet as she replaced empty beer pitchers with full ones.

"Yeah," I agreed, leaning forward to scratch Hades' ears. "She wasn't here last time."

"Nope. I'd remember an ass like that, no matter how fucked up I was." He grinned. "She looks Latina, too. You know how long it's been since I had a woman of my own culture?"

"I dunno, two weeks?" I scoffed.

"Exactly. Too long."

His eyes followed her as she came to our table, although hers remained low and focused on her tasks at hand.

"Excuse me." Jandro reached out to catch her wrist, making her flinch but she didn't pull away. Smart girl.

"*Como se llama?*" he asked for her name in his mother tongue.

She lifted her hazel eyes to him, her gaze flickering to me for a moment before answering his question.

"Mariposa," she answered.

Jandro grinned broadly, his fingers sliding from her wrist to the inside of her palm. I suppressed an eyeroll. The man was far too flirtatious than necessary. Any one of us in the Steel Demons could bed a woman without much effort, but my Latin VP treated it like an art form.

"Mariposa," he repeated, tasting her name in his mouth. "And what's a pretty little butterfly like you doing in a place like this?"

"I'm actually a medic," she answered, straightening her spine. "I'm just passing through, helping out while I stay here."

"Medic?" I repeated, not bothering to hide my surprise. "A *female* medic?"

"That's right," she returned her gaze to me. "I was educated before the law passed."

My eyebrows lifted. Even years before the Collapse, women being educated was a rarity. As their rights were gradually stripped away, girls of high school age and even younger were kidnapped and never seen again. The few who escaped and tried to press charges got laughed out of the courtrooms. Then it became illegal in most jurisdictions for a woman to file a criminal case without a reliable male witness.

Frightened parents started keeping their daughters locked away at home. While temporarily safer this way, it didn't exactly provide them with tools to survive a post-Collapse society. Once the border wars broke out, every home, car, and business was a pillaging free-for-all. Safety simply didn't exist anymore.

Survival was no longer a right. It was a privilege to be earned, as I and the men of my club knew all too well.

"Now, Mariposa," Jandro leaned back, still holding her hand and causing her to lean over the table. "We've had a long, exhausting ride. What'll you take for a full body examination with those skilled hands of yours?"

Her expression morphed from apprehensive to hardened determination within a second. She snatched her hand from Jandro's grip and straightened up.

"I don't deal in sex. There's plenty of girls here who provide that."

Jandro smirked. "It wasn't a yes or no question. Everyone has a price. Just name yours."

"The answer is still no." She grabbed our empty pitchers and charcuterie board. "I'll bring you more food and drink."

Jandro chuckled to himself as she beelined back toward the kitchen. "She has no idea who she's saying no to. Good thing I like a challenge."

"Have fun with that," I muttered, rolling my neck around on my shoulders.

For the last fifty miles or so, I'd been looking forward to getting off the bike and burying my cock in a woman. But now that I was here, a night of long, uninterrupted sleep sounded much better. Although Jandro's proposition of a full-body rub down didn't sound bad. Unfortunately, I too preferred it from Mariposa the pretty medic. As President, I had every right to claim her for myself but I wasn't petty enough do that to my VP.

Even so, the thought turned over in my head as I watched her slicing cheese and meats through the open kitchen doors. She'd taken off her windbreaker and her bare shoulders looked small enough for me to wrap my whole hands around. Her neck was long and graceful, a few shades lighter than Jandro's tan.

"You ready for me, Reaper baby?"

My view was blocked yet again by yet another unwelcome service girl crawling into my lap. Jandro hid his laugh by swiping some of Gunner's beer from the next table. Gun's falcon, Horus, screeched and flapped his wings in annoyance, to which Jandro promptly flipped him the bird.

Hades growled with irritation at my feet, echoing my feelings exactly as the girl turned to face me, straddling my thighs as she ground herself against my very unexcited dick.

"Let's go up to my room," she mewled, bouncing in my lap. "You can lay back and just let me ride you. I won't make ya work, baby."

And that was exactly what made me stay soft. I didn't chase skirt like Jandro did, but desperation was always a turn-off. Especially from a whore.

"I haven't eaten a damn meal yet," I growled, shoving her off just hard enough to get my point across. "Your pussy is not the fucking holy grail."

She quickly composed herself, smoothing out her flimsy dress and lowering her eyes demurely.

"Jandro?" she inquired almost shyly.

"Sorry, babe. I have different tastes tonight. Here's an idea, though." He pointed down the length of the couches to the man closest to the door. "Why don't you give Shadow some love? He hasn't gotten any in a while."

The girl wrinkled her nose with displeasure. "The big, scarred one? He's scary."

"You ought to be a lot more scared of us," I warned her. Jandro nodded in agreement.

She looked back and forth between us and Shadow a few times, chewing her lip. "He's just not as handsome as you two and Gunner, though. And Gunner says I'm not his type," she whined.

"You fuck men for smokes and liquor," I snapped at her. "Before the Collapse, you would have fucked for money. If you're gonna beg, don't be a chooser."

She shrank back as I raised my voice at her, and finally scurried away. Jandro shook his head at me as he laughed quietly. I reached down to pet Hades again, only to find my dog was no longer at my side.

"What the—? Hades!" I looked around, no sign of my four-legged beast anywhere. He never left my side unless I gave him a command. If one of these service bitches actually fucking did something to him...

Next to me, Jandro just chuckled. "Looks like we're

not the only ones who want to sniff out Miss Mariposa."
He nodded toward the kitchen and I followed his gaze.

As the leader of the most notorious MC in the Southwest, I saw a lot of weird shit before, during, and after the Collapse. But I never saw anything like what played out before my eyes that very moment.

Hades had walked right up next to Mariposa as she chopped cheese cubes and salami. He stared at her intently while she appeared to be talking to him in a low voice. Then he sat.

My dog fucking *sat* for another human being. To add insult to injury, he tilted his head and licked his greedy lips as she held a cheese cube a few inches in front of his nose. The morsel of food grew closer and closer to him until he scarfed it off of her fingers.

And if that wasn't enough, he licked her hand and allowed her to scratch his head. No one, not even men in my own club, had been permitted to touch him that way.

I raised that dog since finding him in a pile of rubble next to an abandoned house. We were cleaning up and scavenging after a border battle, and heard something like a baby screaming bloody murder. He could fit in the palm of my hand and those little puppy lungs wouldn't shut the hell up. Not until after we raided a vet clinic down the road and I got my hands on some puppy formula.

I'd never cared for an animal in my life, so I wasn't sure what brought me to hold onto the little mutt rather than put him out of his misery. All I knew was Hades and I developed a bond closer to friendship between people, rather than animal and owner. Gunner told me he felt similarly when he found Horus as a chick.

I found Hades a few months after losing Daren, so I chalked it up to filling the void that my little brother left behind. That was a year ago, and Hades had been loyal and protective only to me since the beginning. He even guarded me while I slept and saved our asses from being ambushed several times. So imagine my shock when he just wandered off to get a piece of cheese from some girl we'd never seen before.

"Hades!" I bellowed loud enough for the whole place to hear me.

The damn dog finally turned to look at me, still licking his chops from his treat like he did nothing wrong.

"Get your ass over here, mutt."

As he trotted back to my side, my eyes lifted to catch Mariposa's once again, before she turned her back to continue her work.

MARIPOSA

Tom wasn't kidding about these bikers having voracious appetites. They drank the beer and ate all the meat and cheese we put out faster than we could refill them. When the service girls came down from their rooms in their high heels and flimsy dresses that left little to the imagination, the Steel Demons consumed them with their eyes just as greedily. Some of them, anyway.

Reaper didn't seem interested in the girl practically humping his leg, nor did the Hispanic man who sat next to him. But I felt their eyes on me far more than was comfortable, and it made my skin crawl.

You're new here. They're curious and are probably going to test how much shit you'll take. Just do your job and roll with it.

I slammed the tap handle back with more force than necessary just before the beer sloshed dangerously close to the pitcher's rim. This was actually *not* my job. This was why I went into debt for a top-tier nursing degree— so I wouldn't become a walking piece of meat for men to ogle. Tension and conflict had been brimming for years before the Collapse. Everyone knew war was coming, and I wanted to help in a way that was meaningful.

A high-pitched squeal and the sound of flesh slapping pulled my attention away from my painstaking care not to spill any beer as I walked. Next to the blonde man with the falcon on his shoulder, a woman was already riding the cock of a fellow biker. She bounced on him with gusto, putting in the work while the man she rode all but ignored her, talking to the blonde man next to him as if this was a completely normal occurrence.

The man sitting on the other side of the sex rodeo polished off his beer pitcher and scooted closer to the cowgirl. He smacked her ass once to get her attention, which had been on the blonde man. When she turned her head to look at who spanked her, he said something and put a hand over his crotch. She leaned over, yanked down his zipper, and proceeded to suck him loudly while still bouncing on the first guy. It was like a trainwreck I couldn't stop myself from watching.

"Get in on this, Gunner! Her asshole's free," laughed the guy getting his dick sucked, stretching his arms wide along the back of the couch.

The blonde man shook his head with an amused chuckle and said something I couldn't hear, the falcon on his shoulder ruffling its feathers as its sharp eyes darted all over the room.

Someone poked me in the back, startling me out of watching the debauchery happening before my eyes.

"Don't watch like that," Gretchen muttered. "They'll think you want to join in."

Ugh, no thanks. It had been over a year since I'd gotten laid, but being used by rough, manhandling outlaws did not sound like fun. I put a birth control implant in my arm just a few months ago, so I was cleared on that front. But the nurse in me was all too aware of the rise of STIs and physical injuries from widespread rape and using sex as currency since the Collapse. At least a third of my patients had some sort of infection or physical trauma related to sex. I could only imagine what the emotional and mental impact did to them.

As I fought to ignore the public threesome and keep my feet moving, I couldn't help but notice the four best-looking members of the club were the only ones not participating in the debauchery. I pushed the thought away just as quickly as it came. Those men were probably just holding out for more attractive, expensive whores.

Not even the guy sitting closest to the door, a huge, powerfully-built man with black hair to his collar, had a woman draping off of him. Some of the hair hung over his face to cover his right eye, and I thought I got a glimpse of some scarring on his forehead. He didn't touch the beer in front of him or talk to anyone. The service girls almost seemed to purposely avoiding him, not that he appeared to care. He just ate salami, cheese, and olives with slow, methodical precision, popping each morsel into his mouth and chewing slowly. The muscles in his jaw moved under a dense, but trimmed black beard dusted with a few grey hairs. His chocolate brown, uncovered eye swept across the entire lobby in silent observation.

I caught myself staring once again—he had that ultra-rugged handsome thing going on that I was a total sucker for—and bumped my shin into the coffee table in front of him.

"Oh shit, I'm sorry!"

I pulled a dish rag from my back pocket and quickly wiped up the beer that sloshed onto the table. My heart crashed against my sternum as I kept my eyes glued to the mess I made. I had no idea if these guys liked to torture or kill their service people for making mistakes, and hoped I didn't just make my first day here my last.

Once the spill was quickly absorbed by my rag, the large man in front of me said nothing. I dared to look up at him and wished I hadn't. His scowl made Reaper's look like a joyful grin.

"Sorry about that," I repeated, praying I wasn't digging myself into a deeper hole. My eyes flickered back down to the nearly full beer pitcher in front of him. "I can take that and get you something else if you prefer?" It would save me a trip from filling up yet another empty pitcher.

He didn't answer—not with words, in any case. His lip curled with disgust, like I was a piece of dog shit on his boot, then flung his hand out toward me as if to say, *get out of my sight and take this shit away.*

I grabbed the pitcher's handle and made off for the next table, where another one of these animals might appreciate it more. Keeping my eyes focused on my work and *not* on the threesome still happening on the next couch, I swapped the full pitcher for an empty one when a hand snapped out and grabbed my wrist.

"Como se llama?" a warm voice asked me.

I looked up. Big mistake. Now I couldn't look away from the hazel eyes so similar to mine. His fingers on my wrist were strong and calloused, but the skin along his muscular arm was smooth and the color of caramel. The smile he wore was far too charming. I had no doubt this man was not only good at breaking hearts, but treated it like a sport. In the bedroom, he probably recited takeout menus in Spanish, making women think he uttered proclamations of love and romance while in the throes of passion.

That smile and the confidence to touch me showed all the signs of a man who wanted to play with more than just a woman's body. Giving him my name like he asked would already be too much. Men didn't care about asking for names or getting to know someone anymore, not when they could just take what they wanted.

And he knew that. He touched on a pre-Collapse custom, knowing such a small gesture would make me feel a little bit like a human again. It was all part of his game, and yet I couldn't resist giving it to him.

"Mariposa," I answered.

His eyes flashed with recognition at the word as his smile grew brighter. It was a look I saw often whenever introducing myself to Spanish speakers. My name meant butterfly, but I unfortunately never got a good grasp of the language. Dad was never around enough to teach me.

"Mariposa," the biker repeated, clearly pleased. His

cut read **VICE PRESIDENT.** "And what's a pretty little butterfly like you doing in a place like this?"

"I'm actually a medic," I said, hoping to squash any nefarious ideas he might be having. "I'm just passing through, helping out while I stay here."

"Medic?"

My eyes slid over to see Reaper's intense green gaze leveled on me again. Jesus, these men had zero qualms about unabashedly staring.

"A *female* medic?" he repeated, eyes sliding over me like trying to figure out how a dude could crossdress so well.

I bristled at his skepticism. It wasn't *that* long ago that women were outlawed from medical jobs in over 80% of post-Collapse territories.

"That's right," I answered, lifting my chin slightly. "I was educated before the laws passed."

"Now, Mariposa." The vice president leaned back into the couch, pulling me forward across the coffee table like he fully expected me to tumble into his lap. He smelled like motor oil and smoke, though not entirely unappealing. "What'll you take for a full-body examination with those skilled hands of yours?"

So much for deterring him. There was a girl getting fucked on the next couch over, why would he bother with me? I snatched my hand away and was surprised at how easily he let go.

"I don't deal in sex," I hissed. "There's plenty of girls here who provide that."

"It wasn't a yes or no question," he remarked, eyes

flashing playfully. "Everyone has a price. Just name yours."

Fuck you and the bike you rode in on. I am not playing your game, pig.

"The answer is still no." I grabbed the empty beer pitcher and food plate, fighting every instinct to throw them right at his smug, grinning face. "I'll bring you more food and drink."

My hands shook so hard, I nearly dropped the dishes on the counter when I made it back to the kitchen. My heart beat erratically and my feet were already sore from the constant running around. The likelihood of making it through the next two weeks seemed abysmally low. There was no avoiding these men, so I could only hope they'd be gone in the next day or two and grow bored of me during that time.

With a shaky breath, I picked up a knife and began cutting into a cheese block. I just had to make it through tonight. Then the next night. Then the one after that. *You'll survive. You'll survive.*

I became so entranced in my cheese-cubing, I nearly jumped out of my skin when something cold and wet nudged my arm.

"Ah! What?" I blinked down at a face with two round dark eyes, pointed ears, and a smiling toothy mouth with a pink tongue lolling out.

"What are you doing here?" I demanded Reaper's dog like he could answer. Hades, I think he called him.

Up close, the animal was even bigger than I initially thought. His shoulder came up to my waist. Sleek muscles across his chest and a glossy coat showed he was well taken care of, neither thin nor overweight. That, at least, was a relief. I'd seen companion animals in far worse conditions since the Collapse. When most people could barely feed themselves or their children, animals always suffered the worst.

"Go away." I made a shooing motion but the dog only stepped closer, nudging my arm out of the way to reach his prize on the counter—cheese.

"Damn it, dog." I covered the food with my hand, looking over my shoulder to see his owner preoccupied with a service girl in his lap.

Hades licked his lips and tilted his head at me as if to say, *See? He'll never know. Just one little piece? Pwease?*

"This is all you get," I said, holding up a cheese cube between my thumb and forefinger. "But you better not get me in trouble with your human, okay?"

Hades' eyes brightened as he lowered his haunches to the floor like a good boy. I stood stunned for a moment. This dog looked like he would have ripped my throat out the moment he walked in next to his owner. Now he was working the puppy dog eyes and begging for treats like he grew up with a sweet old lady.

"Please don't bite my fingers off," I muttered as I slowly held the cheese out to him.

To my relief, only his tongue touched my hand as he scarfed down the cube in two big, chomping bites. It brought a smile to my face for the first time in weeks. He looked like such a sweet puppy for a moment. I forgot about who he came with and what those big eyes must have witnessed his owner do. In that one innocent moment, I allowed myself to reach out and tentatively scratch one of his ears.

"Hades!" The yell came from across the room and made me flinch. "Get your ass over here, mutt."

The dog trotted back to lay at his owner's feet, Reaper's unforgiving gaze holding me rooted to my spot. Fuck. He must have seen me feed him and pet him. The sick, churning feeling in my stomach told me the Steel Demons president wouldn't take kindly to someone touching his pet.

Turning back to my chopping, I struggled to calm the fearful, ragged breaths in and out of my chest as Reaper's eyes felt like daggers in my back.

MARIPOSA

I woke up the next morning to a line of prostitutes outside my door. Not for anything fun, considering I don't swing that way.

Nope, they heard what I offered and came to receive my services. I got a cup of stale coffee from the kitchen, tied my hair back, opened my pack, and got down to work.

Most of them wanted birth control, as expected. Thankfully I stocked up from the pharmacy I stayed at before coming here. I had pills, patches, rings, implants, and IUDs up the wazoo.

The majority of them preferred the implant like the one I had in my arm. It lasted for three years and was relatively easy to insert and remove. Pills were too easy to lose, forget, or be tampered with. IUDs were invasive and more painful to insert, plus I was not the best at putting them in. While in school, my dream was to be a labor and delivery nurse. I wanted to catch babies as they came out, not shove things back in.

But at this point in my post-Collapse medic career, most of my skills came from straight-up winging it. I'd never implanted a birth control device before until I put my first one in my arm. I never performed any kind of surgery myself until I had to dig shrapnel out of a kid's thigh at the old Texas-New Mexico border.

Sometimes I was lucky enough to learn from other medics on the road. Former doctors, nurse practitioners, and physician's assistants all gave me tricks of the trade I never would have learned in a pre-Collapse job. They made me realize how vital it was to share skills in a world like this. One day I could be pulling a dead tooth from a guy's mouth and the next day, giving methadone to a drug addict. To be truly useful, we had to adapt to everything.

In between birth control implants and morning-after pills, some of the girls talked to me about physical symptoms they were feeling. A few were embarrassed, understandably so, but I heard it all before. I handed out antibiotics and could only hope their infections weren't the kind that resisted medication. With no reliable labs around, I couldn't do blood or urine tests to verify anything.

My line finally started to go down around midmorning, and my stomach cramped from hunger. I knew there was some leftover stew from the Steel Demons' dinner last night. I yearned for flavorful broth and hearty potatoes by the time the last woman sat down on my bed.

"My stomach's been hurting," she whined, holding her forearm low against her abdomen. I recognized her as the girl having sex on the couch with the two bikers yesterday.

"Okay, for how long?" I asked, snapping on a fresh pair of gloves.

"I dunno, three days?"

I stared at her. "You've been in pain like this for *three days* and still offered your services to those men last night?"

"Save the judgment, bitch," she hissed, teeth grinding in pain. "Last night guaranteed food and clothes for my daughter for another two weeks. Besides," her eyes flashed with hard determination, "if I stayed up in my room, one of them would have come up and found me. And those men aren't the kind you can say no to."

"I'm sorry, I wasn't trying to judge," I sighed with a small shake of my head. When did humanity become such a shithole? "May I touch you?"

She allowed me to press gently on her stomach while I asked all the routine questions. I had my suspicions but after just a few minutes of examining her, I was all but certain.

"What's your name?" I pulled my hands away from her and sat up.

"Kitty," she answered, fear creeping into her eyes. "What's wrong with me?"

"Kitty, your stomach's fine. But my suspicion is you have an ovarian cyst. With your permission, I'd like to perform a pelvic exam to make sure."

Her eyes widened. "What the hell is that?"

"An ovarian cyst is a growth on one of your ovaries

that can cause pain and cramping. They're usually benign, meaning not cancerous, but carry a risk of rupturing, which can cause internal bleeding and severe pain. Sexual intercourse, especially if it's rough, can increase the risk of a rupture."

"And you want to do what?"

"A pelvic exam," I replied clinically. "I'll need to insert two fingers in your vagina and put pressure around your lower abdomen for a few seconds to examine your uterus, fallopian tubes, and ovaries."

Kitty scooted away from me, a grimace of disgust on her face. "I don't do chicks."

"Neither do I. There's nothing sexual about this," I told her. "It's purely medical. But it's also your body. I won't do anything without your permission."

She hesitated, nearly doubled over with pain. "And if it is that thing you said? Then what?"

"Considering how much pain you're in," I chewed my lip, always hating this part, "I think removal of the cyst would be the best option."

"Removal?! How?"

"With surgery," I said as gently as I could. "It's a relatively minor surgery, although that depends on the size and where exactly the cyst is located. And I need to do the pelvic exam to find that out."

Kitty's face paled as she scrambled off on my bed, heading for the door as she clutched her stomach. "Fuck no! You are *not* touching my pussy and you sure as fuck are *not* cutting me open!"

I nodded, completely unsurprised at her reaction. "Let me know if you change your mind, Kitty." I began cleaning up my supplies. "I'll be here for two more weeks. I just want to help."

She left my room, muttering to herself about fucking dykes while I threw all my used gloves and wrappers into a plastic bag and tied it off. Years ago, she would have offended me. I remembered the helpless feeling of trying to make a fellow woman understand that examining her was part of my job. The more I tried to explain it to her, the more she freaked out. I almost *did* feel like some kind of predator, even though I only wanted to help.

An OB/GYN consoled me after that, reminding me that consent and respect for our patients' autonomy was paramount in today's world. Above all else, people needed to feel like they could trust us, and that meant backing off when they said no. Even if their lives were at risk.

I cleaned everything off my bed and began tidying up before heading down to eat, when a small voice came from my open doorway.

"Mari?"

I whirled around. "Gretchen!" I gasped, stunned at the girl's face.

She had two black eyes and a split lip caked in dried blood. Bruises covered her neck, arms, and probably more places I couldn't see. It took all my self-control to quell the rage within me. Choosing the life of a prostitute was one thing, but she was just a kid, for fuck's sake.

"Come here, sweetie." I sat on the bed and patted the spot next to me. "Who did this?"

"It doesn't matter," she rasped, allowing me to feel

gently around her face. No broken bones as far as I could tell.

"Did those fucking bikers attack you?" I got up to rummage through my pack for pain relievers.

"Don't worry about me, Mari. I'm used to it," she gave a weak smile that broke my heart. "But do you have any, ah, morning-after pills left?"

Of course, I knew before she said it. But for some reason, her saying those words hit me like a sledge-hammer to the chest. I'd treated dozens of sexual assault victims before. Why her asking me that affected me so much, I had no idea. Maybe because she was young with so much potential, or that she'd just escaped the exact same abuse months before. Or it could have been the way she smiled through the pain in her face, as if trying to encourage *me* to chin up and get through the day.

"Gretchen..." I didn't know what to say. My chest felt so heavy. So I just pulled the sealed package of pills from my pack. "Take these right away. Both at the same time. You might feel some side effects—"

"Thanks, Mari. I'll pay you back in some way. I don't have much to trade but I can clean your room or—"

"Don't, please. You don't owe me anything." I sat next to her on the bed, taking her small hands between mine. "Do you want to come with me when I leave?" The question tumbled out faster than I could think about it. All I could focus on was keeping this girl safe and far away from the brutal men probably sleeping in the rooms right next to ours.

Her eyes brightened with hope. "Really? Can I?"

It was too late to go back on my word now, so I nodded. "We'll be safer together. I can teach you basic medic skills, too."

"That would be amazing, Mari!" She glanced nervously toward my open door as sounds from the other rooms floated down the hallway. It was nearly noon and sounded like the Steel Demons were just rising.

"We shouldn't say anything to Tom and Liza," she whispered. "I told them I'd be staying a lot longer and...they wouldn't understand."

"My lips are sealed," I told her, making a zipping motion over my mouth. "And hey, if any of those bikers try to mess with you, yell for me. I'm pretty handy with a scalpel."

"I will," she nodded. "But they probably want nothing to do with me now, looking like this."

"Let's hope they leave both of us alone, but still," I gave her shoulder a gentle squeeze. "Just be careful."

———

GRETCHEN WANTED to go down to the kitchen with me, but I insisted she rest in her room until at least it was time to cook dinner.

"Doctor's orders," I told her sternly, fluffing her pillows up behind her head.

"You're not a doctor," she teased back with a smile. How she could still bring herself to joke around was beyond me.

"Medic's orders, then," I tapped her nose. "I'll bring you some lunch."

"Fine," she sighed, relaxing back at last.

Perhaps it was naive of me to think the Steel Demons wouldn't be milling about the place like they owned it, but the last thing I expected to see was one of them reading a book in the lobby.

And not just any book. The Bible.

The blonde one with hair to his collarbone, his falcon perched on his shoulder as it preened its feathers, studied the thin pages in front of him like the surrounding world didn't exist.

His long legs stretched out in front of him, leather boots propped up on the coffee table as his blue eyes moved, entranced by ancient prophecies transcribed hundreds if not thousands of times.

Like with the big scarred guy last night, I was so fixed on staring at him that my clumsy ass walked right into the kitchen doors with a hard *thunk* to my forehead.

"Fuck!" I slapped my palms to my head, knowing getting through unnoticed was impossible now.

"Take it easy," the blonde biker grinned at me. "There are better ways to cure a hangover."

"Not hungover," I grumbled, pushing my way through the door. My cheeks burned and I wanted to forget what had just happened. So when Blonde Biker and his falcon followed me into the kitchen, I wished to sink into the floor from embarrassment and fear.

"Can I help you?" I asked apprehensively, moving to put the counter between me and him.

"Coffee would be great. There's none in my room

and not a soul down here 'til you headbutted the door."
He shot me a cocky grin.

"Uh, okay." I turned slowly toward the cabinets, keeping my eyes on him. "I'll make some."

"Thanks, *Marrriposa.*" He said my name with an exaggerated rolling r and Spanish accent. "My boy Jandro couldn't stop saying your name last night. I'm Gunner, by the way. This is Horus." He pointed to the bird on his shoulder.

I couldn't think of what to say. *Pleased to meet you* would have been an obvious lie. *Your hair is pretty* would give him the wrong idea. So I opted for an awkward joke.

"Does Horus want coffee, too?" I started cringing before the words ever left my mouth.

Gunner threw his head back and laughed, clutching his flat stomach like it was the funniest thing he heard all day. A smile peeked at the corner of my mouth before I could stop myself.

"Nah, he's a fancy bastard and likes his tea," Gunner winked when he could breathe. "But seriously, he caught a big breakfast this morning. A nice fat gopher, didn't you, boy?"

He scratched the bird under its wickedly curved beak and my smile grew. How long had it been since I just had a silly conversation with a cute guy? Gunner almost seemed normal, if even nice. He looked just like a guy at my college campus I would flirt with, pre-Collapse. I'd even let him buy me a drink.

Then my eyes fell to his leather cut and reality slapped the smile right off my face. The patch on the left side depicted two crossed assault rifles with "2A" beneath them. I didn't know much about MC life, but I knew 2A referred to the Second Amendment of the United States, a law that no longer existed in this gigantic land mass which didn't even have a name anymore.

2A became an emblem for those that thrived on the new violent, chaotic nature of modern society. Those who wore it lived for the bloodlust of the border wars, the power of taking someone's life with a handheld machine. They lived and breathed death and violence.

Because the Second Amendment, once central to American culture, was the right to bear arms.

If that wasn't enough, a long bandolier of ammunition stretched from Gunner's shoulder to his hip. I don't know how I missed it before, but the kitchen lights made the bullets gleam like endless rows of small, golden missiles.

A black handgun sat in a holster on his opposite hip, and there was no telling how many other weapons he had on him. This easy-smiling, angelic-looking man absolutely *loved* violence.

"How about that coffee, Mari?" he teased, resting a hand on the weapon at his hip. "Can I call you Mari? Not that *Marrriposa* isn't pretty. It's just a hell of a mouthful."

"Uh, sure." I turned uneasily toward the coffee pot, fumbling for cups with shaking hands. "Call me whatever you like."

"In that case, I might call you Maripos-*ass*, 'cause *damn*, mami."

In two steps, he was right behind me. I froze at the heat of his breath on my neck. My eyes squeezed shut, bracing myself for his hands on me, and then the gun or knife that would surely follow.

"Relax," his lips brushed my ear as fingertips trailed across my waist. "You're shaking like a leaf. I'll make it good for you, baby girl."

His thick erection pressing against my ass stole a gasp from my mouth. Gunner let out a groan in reply, his lips falling to my neck as he held my waist in place. My core roared like an inferno, my touch-starved body leaning into his heat and hardness as if of it's own will, but that didn't stop the frantic thoughts.

At least he's not doing this to Gretchen. At least she's safe upstairs. I'll survive this.

"Screeeeech!"

Horus, still on Gunner's shoulder, suddenly began flapping his wings and screaming bloody murder. Temporary relief flooded me as Gunner pulled away.

"Go away, Horus. I'm busy," he chastised the bird with a swat of his hand, but the falcon would not let up. His talons curled into the worn leather at Gunner's shoulder, holding on and screeching in his human's face.

"...Mari?"

"Gretchen!" Hot shame filled me as her swollen, bruised eyes widened with fear, peeking through the gap in the swinging kitchen door.

She took in Gunner standing so close to me and seemed to understand exactly what was about to happen.

"I told you to rest," I blurted out, my heart pounding

wildly. In truth, I could have kissed her with gratitude for showing up right then.

"I came down to grab some water." Her eyes darted nervously toward Gunner, who stared back at her intensely.

"I'll bring you some," I said quickly. "And some food. Go on back up. I'll be right there."

She nodded and retreated back, letting the door close softly.

"Holy shit," Gunner turned back to me, bewilderment on his face. "What the fuck happened to her?"

I glared at him, unable to help myself. "Like you don't know."

His eyes widened in shock before narrowing venomously at me in return. "Look. I know what I look like, but I do *not* fucking beat up little girls. No one in the SDMC does that shit."

"Okay, Gunner," I said placidly. "If you don't mind, I'd like to make coffee and lunch unmolested. Thank you."

I turned back to the coffee machine without waiting for an answer, although still fully expecting a gun or knife in my back.

Instead, I heard the ruffling of feathers as Horus finally calmed down, then Gunner's booted feet walking away and out the kitchen doors.

FIVE

JANDRO

I drummed my fingers on the long conference table stretched out in front of me. Reaper sat to my left, hands folded calmly in his lap, and Hades lying at his feet like usual. Tom, the owner of this service station, sat across from us, visibly nervous and sweating.

Any man with two brain cells to rub together would have seen this meeting coming, but Tom chose to play dumb. That might have worked with some little wannabe MC, but not with us.

"When we made our protection agreement, I assumed your club would be around to, you know, protect me," Tom whined. "*And* my assets! Just last week, a bunch of masked thugs on dirt bikes rode up and took three of my girls. Expensive ones, too! And where the hell were you guys?"

My fingers closed into a fist as I opened my mouth to retort but Reaper raised a hand, asking me for silence. I closed my trap, fighting my temper to jump to my President and best friend's defense.

"We're not responsible for the consequences of your provocations," Reaper answered him. "You brought this on yourself, Tom. Our agreement was for *protection*, not babysitting and cleaning up your messes."

Tom's face twisted into a well-practiced look of shock. If Hollywood didn't get swallowed by the ocean fifty years ago, he would have been nominated for an Oscar.

"Provocations? I have no idea what you're talking about! I run an honest business! I'm--"

"Shut the fuck up, old man," I snapped. "Don't talk to us like we're fucking idiots. We keep our ears to the ground and word spreads. We know. And everyone in the Southwest is going to learn how honest your business really is."

"What?!"

"I'm sure you can recall our agreement also included discretion. If you forgot, I have the original signed copy right here," Reaper tapped the left side of his cut. "So if you're as honest as you say, why would the bartender at the Shady Lady say you were bragging all night long about having the Steel Demons in your back pocket?"

A flash of panic passed through Tom's watery eyes. "Because she's a lying whore!"

"Or you're a lying sack of shit," I suggested. "You start making claims like that, people are going to test to see if they're true. You're basically the kid on the playground goading everyone with, 'my dad can beat up your dad.'"

"Okay, I might have told a couple of close friends

after I had a few but it wasn't like that! It doesn't mean I deserve to have punks ransacking my business!"

"Actually, that's exactly what it means." Reaper rose to his feet, Hades loyally glued to his side, and I followed. "You agreed to discretion in exchange for reasonable protection. You've broken that agreement so the deal is off."

He started for the door and I fell in after him, leaving Tom to scramble desperately after us from the other side of the room.

"Wait! I haven't broken anything! I kept my side of the bargain! You have garages for your bikes, all the food you can eat, women to fuck, all because of me!"

I whipped around and thrust my palm in the center of Tom's chest, making him stumble back with fear in his eyes.

"You accuse my president of lying again and you're a dead man," I threatened in a low voice. "You're lucky to still be breathing right now after breaking a deal with us."

As Tom shivered like a chihuahua, Reaper turned slowly to face him again.

"Everything you provide, we can easily find some-where else. But you'll never have the protection of an MC again, because they'll all know you can't be trusted."

Tom's mouth flopped open like a fish, glub-glubbing uselessly. I felt no sympathy for the bastard. He of all people should have known that in this world, where everything could be taken in an instant, a man's word was the most valuable thing he had.

I slapped him on the shoulder and gave him a shit-eating grin. "We leave before dawn tomorrow. And if it wasn't obvious, we won't be returning next month."

Reaper, Hades, and I left the room, already halfway down the hall and pulling out our cloves to smoke when Tom came tearing down after us.

"Wait!" He nearly tripped over his own feet to reach us. "Please rethink this! You're making a mistake."

"Tom, I don't know if you realized this," Reaper glared, his patience thinning as the black cigarette bobbed between his lips, "But you need us a lot more than we need you. It's not our fault you fucked it up."

"I know, I know. If you could just, maybe," he rubbed his shiny forehead, grasping at straws, "accept a parting gift! As my deepest apology, you can have Kitty. She's one of my best."

"No thanks," I scoffed, flicking open my Zippo to light up right in the hallway. "We aren't lacking in pussy. And even if we were, we prefer a higher quality."

"The kitchen girl, then!" Tom spoke quickly, reeking of desperation. "Gretchen. She's a good cook and young enough that she hasn't been fully broken in yet."

"No," Reaper barked with an air of disgust. "We don't deal in brainwashed children."

"My new girl then." Tom refused to let this go. "She served you last night. She's a medic, although I don't know about her bedroom skills."

"Mariposa," I exhaled her name in a thick cloud of smoke, making Tom cough pathetically.

Reaper said nothing right away. His expression was pensive as he lit up his own cigarette and took a long drag, almost as though he was actually considering it.

Tom looked hopeful for a moment, a grin starting to spread across his face. That was until Reaper's hand shot out, catching the old man by the throat and shoving him against the wall so hard, the back of his head bounced. Hades pinned his ears back, lowering his head and growling with his teeth inches away from Tom's dick.

"No parting gifts. No more deal," Reaper said, low and menacing next to Tom's face. "SDMC is washing our hands of you."

He released Tom's throat and headed for the exit, not looking back as the old man sank to the floor, clutching his throat as he struggled to regain his breath.

Hades and I followed Reaper outside. I leaned against the railing next to him while his dog sat on his haunches. We were on some balcony overlooking a dirty crater in the ground that had once been a pool. Years ago we would smoke just like this and then skateboard in empty pools, hoping to impress girls with our skills. Pre-Collapse life had been so much simpler.

"You almost said yes to the medic," I observed, flicking my ash over the railing. "Why didn't you?"

"Because," he exhaled, "accepting any parting gift would just be a string that keeps us tied to him. If we accept something from him, we'll still owe something in return. Better to cut the strings altogether."

That wasn't the question I asked, and he knew that. Still, I humored him and tried again in another way.

"All of that is true. But we could just steal her."

Reaper hissed in a sharp breath as he dragged on his clove. "No."

"Why not?" I was genuinely surprised by his refusal.

"I thought you wanted a medic for the club after Daren-
-"

"I do. Just not her."

"Bro," I laughed in disbelief. "I dunno if you noticed, but medics aren't exactly growing on trees. She might be the last one we see in a while."

"I'm fine with that. You jerkoffs just need to not die on me in the meantime."

"Okay," I mused. "Humor me, then. Why *not* her? Because she's female?"

"Yes."

"Reaper, my man!" A laugh barked out of me so loud and sudden, it made Hades look at me with his ears pinned back. "Come on, now. We were both adults pre-Collapse, so I know you don't believe that horseshit. Not even twenty years ago, the US had plenty of female doctors, lawyers—"

"I'm sure she can do the job," Reaper snapped, stroking Hades' forehead. "But have you thought about what an educated woman in the club will mean? We might as well paint targets on our backs."

"We already do, essentially," I pointed out. Half the clubs in the Southwest wanted to join us, the other half wanted us wiped off the map. We bled for every square inch of territory we took and earned every whisper of our reputation. That kind of fame made us heroes to some and an obstacle to others.

"It's not just making us a target," Reaper leaned closer to me. "Educated women get ideas. They're dangerous because they want to change things. We need a man who can fall in line with club politics and not be a constant thorn up my ass."

"I hear you, bro," I nodded, tossing my cigarette butt into the empty pool. "I understand. I just know how hard it was for you to lose Daren—"

"I swear to God, Jandro, get the fuck off my nutsack."

"I am, man, for real. I'm just saying the whole club lost a brother, not just you. I figured finding any medic, male or female, would give you some peace of mind that we won't lose someone like that again."

"I am at peace. It happened. There's nothing we can do about it." He flung his cigarette into the pool, the stiffness in his arm showing he was all but at peace with his little brother's death. But I didn't mention it again. That was his own demon to wrestle with.

"*Nothing* like that is going to happen again," he said. "Having a medic would just be an insurance policy. Whoever we find needs to fit in with the club, first and foremost. They need to be trustworthy above all."

"And you don't think a woman can be trusted?"

"Fuck no," he barked. "If the Collapse fucked us over as badly as it fucked them, I wouldn't trust my own goddamn shadow."

"You make a good point," I chuckled, pulling out another slim black cigarette.

Reaper and I barely lit up our second smokes when Hades rose stiffly from his sitting position. His ears pricked forward as he pointed through the balcony railing to the pool deck below.

"Easy, boy," Reaper assured him gently.

Within seconds, Gunner and Horus came into view. Our blonde arms dealer and captain of the guard usually had a sunny disposition about him, but his face was pinched into a frown as he walked hurriedly toward us alongside the pool.

"Been looking all over for you fucks," he yelled up irritably.

Horus released his shoulder with a screech, flying the short distance toward us until he grabbed the balcony railing in his talons. Hades, now relaxed at the sight of his feathered friend, placed his front paws on either side of the falcon to stand on his hind legs. I swore that dog never stopped growing. At this height, he was almost taller than me and Reaper.

"What's the matter, Gun?" Reaper reached around to scratch his Doberman's belly.

Gunner huffed out a sigh and looked up at us grimly. "I gotta talk to you guys about something."

MARIPOSA

"You really should be resting," I grumbled, watching Gretchen carry a twenty-pound bag of rice across the kitchen.

"And leave you to do everything yourself? No way, Jose!" She cut open the bag and began dumping its contents into a large pot. "I'll just work back here while you serve drinks and stuff if you don't mind. They prefer a pretty face to look at, or at least not a fucked up one."

I simmered in my anger as I sliced through cheese and salami for the Steel Demons' appetizers. We had no ice for the swelling on Gretchen's face, although cool towels and Tylenol helped somewhat. She was obviously still in pain by the way she worked. I had no idea why she insisted on waiting hand and foot on the men who did this to her, rather than rest and wait it out until they were gone.

"Why don't Tom and Liza ever help out?" I asked. "This is their place, after all."

"Tom would never do women's work," Gretchen muttered, now dumping water over the rice. "And Liza's lost too many brain cells to do anything. She's probably high out of her mind on fentanyl right now."

"Perfect," I muttered, arranging the cheese and meat on a board. "What would they even do without us?"

"Find other girls. We're replaceable like machines, after all."

No, we're not. We're fucking people. But I kept my mouth shut as I headed out to the lobby—food board in one hand, pitcher of beer in the other.

Being the only one running food and drinks out, I had to hustle extra fast. Sweat collected on my brow and my feet never stopped moving. The bikers were just as voracious eaters and drinkers as the first night, although this time felt different.

The men were quieter, talking to each other in low voices and all but ignoring the service girls. Tension hung in the air like the first moments before a fight. Even Reaper's dog seemed more vigilant than normal.

I looked for Kitty among the bored and rejected service girls, but she was nowhere to be seen. Chewing my lip in concern, I hoped I'd be able to check on her if I ever got a break tonight.

My rounds took me back to the large man all dressed in black, with his long hair covering one eye. Again he sat by the door, not touching his beer, nor talking to anyone.

"You know, if you don't drink," I paused, balancing my empty tray on my hip, "you could say something and

I won't waste a trip putting a beer pitcher in front of you."

His uncovered brown eye lifted to me, widening slightly as though surprised. Then just as quickly, his gaze snapped back down to the table, fists clenching on his knees. I couldn't help but look at him with curiosity. *Is he* able *to talk? And if not, what made him that way?*

Someone else's hand clapped down on the big man's shoulder, and a charming smile made my pulse quicken.

"Shadow prefers hard liquor." The handsome vice president took a seat next to his silent comrade. "Beer takes too long for this guy to feel anything, and he just ends up pissing like a racehorse the whole night." His bright hazel eyes drank me in seductively. "I don't think I introduced myself. I'm Jandro, Reaper's right hand man."

"Jandro?" I repeated. "So your real name is Alejandro, I take it? Why not just go by that, or Alex, like a normal person?"

It probably wasn't smart of me to get snippy with these guys, but my irritation was at an all-time high. They assaulted a teenage girl, who just wanted to sweep it under the rug, treated women like fuck toys in general, and consumed their collective weight in food and beer for what, exactly? And I was just expected to smile, look pretty, and give whatever they asked? Fuck that.

Jandro's grin just spread wider at my dig about his name. "Because I'm not a normal guy, *Marrriposa*. None of us in the SDMC are. Isn't that right, Shadow?"

The large man just grunted as he popped a cheese cube in his mouth and chewed.

"Let me guess," I mused. "You're Shadow because you're tall, dark, and silent?"

He didn't answer, as expected, but I was kind of hoping he would look up at me again. Something about this large, silent man piqued my curiosity.

"You're not far off," Jandro answered instead. "He's also our last line of defense. Shadow rides in the rear, watching our backs because nothing gets past him."

"Well, if it makes you any happier, Shadow," I shifted my trays to my opposite hip. "I think we have some whiskey in the back."

That did it. He looked at me again, just for a brief moment before jerking his gaze back down.

Jandro chuckled, nudging his friend's arm. "*Tu eres un angel, Mariposa.*"

My chest fluttering more than it should, I just nodded and turned back to the kitchen. As I walked away, I swore I overheard Jandro saying something like, "See? Not all women are..."

Once again, I dropped off empties in the kitchen and returned with stocked platters and full drinks, including a fifth of whiskey for Shadow. My feet and arms screamed at me but I was doing the work of at least two people and couldn't afford to stop. I only did so when trying to breeze by Reaper and Gunner's table, and the Steel Demons president shot out like a snake to grab my forearm.

"Where's Tom tonight?" he asked, green eyes heavy and intense.

"I don't know," my teeth clenched against his unforgiving grip on my arm. "He owns the place, he could be anywhere."

"I need to see him."

"You're welcome to find him yourself. I'm kind of busy."

"Fine."

He released me so suddenly, I stumbled backwards and nearly fell on my ass. Despite recovering quickly and continuing my rounds to the tables, I felt his gaze on me as heavily as though his hands rested on my shoulders.

Ignoring him as best I could while I worked my tail off, he and his men finally reached a point where they slowed down on their eating and drinking. I took the opportunity to run upstairs to check on Kitty. Something inside had been nagging at me to check on her ever since she came to me this morning. If I focused on nothing else, I swore I could feel a stabbing pain on the lower left side of my abdomen, where my ovary was. I couldn't begin to explain how I knew, but my gut told me that sensation had to do with her.

I didn't know which room was hers, so I walked down the first hallway of doors slowly, listening through the thin wood for any sounds of someone in pain. Muffled moans and groans came through some of them, most likely sex sounds. Then a sharp cry at the end of the hall had me stopping in my tracks.

When I heard it again, I ran to the nearest door and pressed my ear to the wood. My pulse shot up at the sounds of agony on the other side.

"Kitty? It's me, the medic. Can I come in?"

A wail of pain answered me, and I opened the door

to see a woman writhing on the bed, clutching her stomach. At her bedside, a girl of about seven years old sat with her knees up to her chin and tears streaming down her face. They both looked up at me with desperation in their eyes as I approached the bed.

"It hurts so bad," Kitty whimpered, her face screwed up in a mask of pain. "God, make it stop..."

"Kitty," I placed a hand on her cheek to make her look at me. "I can help you. Will you let me?"

"Yes, please! Fuck!"

I turned to the girl, who I suspected was her daughter, and gave her my best reassuring smile. "Hi, sweetie. I'm going to make your mom feel better, but I need my pack. Can you grab it for me? It's down the hall, fourth door on the left."

The girl nodded and took off, then I tried my best to examine Kitty despite her wriggling around.

"I don't care if you cut it out of me," the woman sobbed. "Just make it stop hurting."

"You're not going to feel a thing in just a minute," I promised.

Her daughter returned with my pack seconds later and I got started on Kitty's pain management. Morphine was too damn expensive and I was far from a qualified anesthesiologist. So I pulled out the box of small, metal canisters to give her the next best thing— nitrous oxide.

Within seconds of inhaling, Kitty's body relaxed and she stopped crying out in pain.

"You fixed her!" the little girl shrieked with relief. "Mommy, you're better!"

Kitty's head rolled toward the sound of her daughter's voice, a smile spreading across her lips. "Hi, baby..."

"She's not all better yet," I muttered, working quickly to clean and prep where I felt the cyst. The laughing gas wouldn't last long and Kitty would still be conscious so I couldn't afford to dally.

"This is going to look messy," I warned them. "Don't look down here. And I need you to hold still, Kitty."

"Okay..."

I made a small, surface-level incision and paused, waiting for a reaction from Kitty. When it was clear she didn't feel any pain, I continued, making the best of the poor lighting and less-than-sterile conditions in the room. The cyst was nearly twice the size of her ovary and I let out a huge sigh of relief as I cut that fucker off.

"You're going to be okay, Kitty. Hold still for me." I gave her another dose of nitrous before preparing my surgical thread. "This won't bother you anymore."

"Thank you," she breathed dreamily, high as a kite. "I should have listened to you...this morning..."

"Don't worry about it." I was a master at surgical sutures now and stitched her up quickly, only glancing once out the window.

The bikers came down for dinner around dusk and now it was pitch black outside. I worked on Kitty as quickly as I could, but still lost complete track of time. Poor Gretchen had to be struggling downstairs.

Just as I cleaned the incision and taped a bandage over it, a piercing scream floated down the hallway.

Fuck, Gretchen! It only occurred to me right then how

dangerous it was to leave her alone with men who had already abused her.

I grabbed the hand of Kitty's daughter. "I'll be right back but in case I don't, make sure this stays covered and dry for two days, okay?"

"Um, okay." Fear returned to her once-calm face. "But promise you won't leave us?"

"I can't. I'm sorry."

In the next moment, I flew down the hall back toward the lobby. I realized in hindsight I should have grabbed a scalpel, but all I could think about was reaching Gretchen in time.

An unarmed woman against six members of the most dangerous motorcycle club members in the Southwest? My odds weren't good but I'd give them hell like they'd never seen before.

At least I was able to help Kitty.

The scene laid out before me when I reached the lobby was the last thing I expected to see.

A pool of blood spread slowly across the tiled floor, coming from the lifeless body of Liza. Her eyes and mouth were wide open in horror, fingers still curled and stained red. Where her throat had once been was now a gaping, shredded hole.

My eyes followed the red paw prints that led away from her body to the terrified women huddled together against the wall. Gretchen and the two service girls trembled and cried as Hades, lips pulled back and stained red teeth on display, snarled inches from their faces like he wanted to kill them next.

"Call your fucking dog off!" I ordered, my mouth going faster than my brain. "Don't hurt them!"

"Take it easy, baby girl." The request came from Gunner, a short-barreled shotgun in one hand. "He's not gonna hurt them. Hades is making sure they stay out of harm's way."

"Bullshit! Look what he did!" I cried, thrusting a hand out toward Liza.

I never got a chance to know her, but even if she was a useless junkie like Gretchen said, she didn't deserve to have her throat ripped out by a dog.

"Hades' work was a kindness. She deserved much worse." Reaper's words floated down another hallway as he approached, dragging something, no, *someone*, behind him. "As do you, Tom."

"No!" My voice squeaked out with shock. Tom was bleeding from the head but alive, wheezing with labored breaths. His legs dragged uselessly behind him at odd angles.

With cool indifference, Reaper grabbed a chunk of Tom's white hair, pulling his head back to bare his throat. In his other hand, he brandished a dagger and pressed it to Tom's neck.

"Stop!" I cried, my voice returning to me. "Why the fuck are you doing this? Just, please stop!"

Reaper looked up, his bright green eyes full of curiosity. "You want me to spare his life?"

"Yes," I breathed, my whole body vibrating with adrenaline. "Please, don't kill any more people."

A cruel smirk pulled at his lips. It didn't matter how

attractive he was. In that moment, he was the living embodiment of evil.

He leaned down close to Tom's ear, but I still heard every word.

"Say hello to the devil for me."

Then he pulled the blade across the old man's neck, creating a thin red line that soon began weeping.

"No!"

I ran toward him, not knowing what else to do. My instinct was to heal, to save lives. Death was all around me but I refused to let life slip away without a fight.

Something hard hit me from the side, knocking the wind out of me and sending me tumbling to the floor. My eyes met Tom's, also lying on the floor as he choked on his own blood. Still dizzy and out of breath, I began pulling myself toward him. Four paws clicked across the tile to stand in my way, a menacing growl rumbling right above my head.

Hades, ears pinned back and teeth bared, lowered his head and barked once in my face.

"Fuck you, son of a bitch," I hissed back. The fucking dog must have been the one to run into me, too.

I kept pulling myself forward, fighting to get my legs underneath me. It was probably too late to save Tom, but what kind of medic would I be if I didn't try?

It was no use, though. Teeth grabbed my pant leg and began pulling me backward.

"Let go of me, fucking dog!" I flailed my legs wildly, hoping to kick him in the face, when a human hand wrapped around my arm and yanked me up.

"Let's move." Reaper's hold transferred from my

arm to around my waist, pinning me to his side as he dragged me toward the front door. "Jandro, we good?"

"All bikes are good, boss."

The realization hitting me was like a swinging door crashing right into my face.

"What the fuck?" I tried to squirm against Reaper's side but he was too strong and solidly built. "I'm not coming with you! No, you're not taking me! Let me go!"

"Shadow, tie her up, then hand her back to me." He passed me off to the large silent man who already had a length of rope ready.

"Shadow, please," I begged, my whole body trembling as he bound my wrists and forearms. "Don't do this. Please look at me. I—" my throat tightened into a dry knot but I forced the words out anyway. "I like it when you look at me."

He paused, his dark pupil dilated in the dim light coming from inside the building. Bikes turned on and revved up, chasing away the quiet night with their roaring. I knew my time was limited, so I spilled every last plea that I had.

"I'll do whatever you want but I have to stay here. I'm a medic and I have patients at this center that need me. You can come see me any time but please, don't make me go. I can't go. Please make Reaper understand—"

"Shadow?"

With a grunt, the large man shoved me toward the cold-blooded murderer he called President. I stumbled without the use of my arms and Reaper caught me, holding me for a moment against his chest like we were lovers embracing.

The way he looked at me was anything but loving, though, and knowing what those hands did made me want to scrub his touch off of me for hours.

He dragged me toward his bike, his surrounding men already seated on theirs and waiting for their leader. When I dug my feet into the ground, he picked me up and placed me in his bitch seat.

"I'm going to fall off if I can't hold onto anything!" I cried out as he seated himself in front of me.

"Really now?" he looked at me over his shoulder with feigned interest. "You wouldn't prefer that over riding with us?"

I bit back a sob, looking down sullenly at my bound arms in front of me. I would rather do anything than go with them, but dying or getting run over didn't sound appealing either.

"Scoot forward."

When I looked up, Reaper had pulled another length of rope from inside his cut. I did as he instructed, scooting an inch closer to him.

"Closer."

I kept moving forward in the seat as he barked out commands until my thighs were touching his. He then wrapped the rope around both of our torsos, tying it secure at his chest.

"You're welcome to try throwing us both off," he said coolly just as the thought came to me. "But I wouldn't recommend it."

My hope sank like a stone as he reached for the

handlebars and took his feet off the ground. The bike lurched forward, picking up speed. Fuck, this was really happening. I'd never reach the Canadian border. I'd never see Gretchen again or give her the chance at her own life.

As Reaper took off, he let out a loud, high-pitched whistle. Seconds later, a dark form ran alongside us. Of course it was Hades, but my fear-stricken brain couldn't comprehend the impossibility of it. A dog running leisurely, lips smiling and tongue lolling out with joy, alongside a motorcycle?

No, all I could do was stare at the Steel Demons' skull emblem, grinning mockingly at me from the back of Reaper's cut, as we rode off into the night.

MARIPOSA

I thought of throwing myself and Reaper off that bike no less than a dozen times. But every time I glanced in one of his mirrors and saw the army of bikes behind us, I chickened out.

Hours crawled by and my body protested every passing minute. I was exhausted but too in pain and desperate to survive to sleep. My ass and thighs cried out from soreness. My arms, still bound in front of me, tingled from numbness, and my back and shoulders killed me. The dry air and sand turned my lips, throat, and eyes to sandpaper.

I'd never ridden on a motorcycle in my life, but it seemed innate to these men. Reaper barely moved in his seat, despite my shifting and wiggling from all the aches and pains.

A dark shape and white teeth grinned at me from the darkness alongside us. Hades? He was *still* running next to his master? Some part of my brain knew that wasn't possible for a normal dog, but it wasn't the main thought plaguing me. My main concern was getting the hell off this bike and escaping whatever the Steel Demons had in store for me.

Some time after the darkness of night began lifting, structures popped up on the horizon to break up the endless landscape of desert. The houses, all abandoned or taken over by squatters, were some of the largest I'd ever seen. All at least two stories and relatively new, complete with solar panels that became standard about twenty years ago. The rusted, broken sign of the Ferrari dealership in the distance makes it clear that this was once a wealthy neighborhood.

A sudden flapping of wings near my head jolted me upright. Despite all the noise, pain, and fear, it seemed I did manage to doze off for a second. With my face against the back of Reaper's shoulder no less.

Blinking, my dry eyes made out Gunner's falcon flying ahead of the bikes, the blonde demon himself pulling up next to Reaper.

Helmetless, his hair flew out around his face like a halo as he shot a winning grin at his president.

"Woohoo!" he yelled over the roaring engines, raising a hand in the air. My eyes followed the length of his arm to the assault rifle he waved like a flag. "Morning, boys! Welcome home, Demons!"

He sped up ahead to lead the pack of bikers, his falcon keeping pace with him just as Hades was with Reaper. A long, horizontal black line materialized a quarter mile in front of us. As we rode closer my exhausted, dry eyes watched as the line took on the form of a tall, wrought-iron gate, complete with armed guards. Once the guards spotted Gunner waving his weapon, the gates began to open slowly.

Mounted to one of the gate posts, a black flag with the grinning skull of the Steel Demons' emblem waved like from the mast of a pirate ship. It looked to be laughing at me as Reaper's bike passed underneath it and through the gates.

The houses we passed by earlier looked like rundown shacks compared to the ones inside these gates. This was a small community but every single home was a sprawling mansion. When it came to taking up residence somewhere, apparently the Steel Demons had a taste for the finer things.

Motorcycles, pickup trucks, and a few RV campers filled the massive driveways where Ferraris and Porsches once sat. But aside from the stark contrast between homes and vehicles, the lots looked otherwise well-maintained. Lawns were still manicured, front porches were swept and tastefully decorated, and there was no graffiti on the garage doors or other signs of careless squatting.

Reaper turned off of the main road to a cul-de-sac where a single McMansion overtook more than its fair share of the landscape. He stopped his bike in front of the monstrous house, turning to address the convoy of bikers behind him.

"Church at noon," he yelled over the rumbling engines. "Get a few hours of sleep, but don't be fuckin' late."

The others broke away, assumedly riding off to their own million-dollar homes, if dollars were still worth anything.

Reaper pulled up to the driveway and cut the engine before loosening the rope that tied us together. Sore, stiff, and numb, my limbs cried out in protest at this new allocation of movement. Fire shot up my legs and I was suddenly going down, the pavement coming up fast to slap me.

Strong hands grabbed me at the last moment, righting me up as Reaper began dragging me to the front door.

"Please, no," I rasped through cracked lips, my legs buckling underneath me. "Please just let me go."

"Yeah? Be my guest."

Reaper released me suddenly and I fell hard on my ass. He loomed over me, scowling like a fed up father disciplining his child as he thrust a hand out toward the street.

"Go ahead. See how far you make it on foot in the desert. You'll even get to enjoy the sunrise."

I should have moved. I should have scooted, crawled, or even rolled down his damn driveway, but I remained sitting on the pavement. Because I didn't know which scared me more, him or being out there with no resources. I didn't even have my medic pack.

"I didn't think so," he remarked, pulling me to my feet as he shoved the door open. "Noelle!" His voice echoed off the marble tiled floor and high vaulted ceilings as he dragged me inside. "Noelle! Get your ass up!"

I couldn't even appreciate the finery of his house with him yelling like that. My eyes bounced around the elegant fixtures and furniture only in search of a place to hide.

"What the fuck are you yelling so goddamned early for?" a woman's voice called from the top of an elegant, winding staircase.

"Just get down here," Reaper huffed in reply.

A woman with shocking red hair, clearly dyed, floated down the staircase, her silk robe fluttering around her. Colorful tattoos decorated from her wrists up her forearms and disappearing under her robe sleeves. When she reached the bottom step and approached us with a piercing stare, her eyes looked to be the same green as Reaper's.

"Noelle, put her up in one of the guest suites for now," Reaper sighed, his voice heavy with exhaustion. "I need to sleep before holding church in a few hours."

"Okay, sure. By the way, hi, big brother. Nice to see you, too." She folded her arms across her chest, staring at him crossly. "Thanks for bringing home *another* stray before the ass-crack of dawn."

Hades, who had been silent at this point, approached the woman with a high-pitched whine.

"Yeah, mutt. I'm talking about you," she grumbled, stroking the dog's face.

"I've been riding all fuckin' night, I don't have time for this." Reaper was already crossing the room, pulling off his cut and then his T-shirt before disappearing down a hallway. Hades quickly trotted after him, nails clicking over the pristine tiles.

"Well," Noelle placed her hands on her hips, examining me from head to toe. "I'd prefer sleep, too, but guess you're my problem now. Come on up." She began ascending the staircase, throwing me a look over her shoulder when I remained rooted to my spot. "Or just stay there, it makes no difference to me. I assume you want a bath, though. Plus some food and water. Maybe a bed?"

My dry tongue darted out to lick my equally parched lips. I was still too tired, too scared, too fucking confused to make sense of whether I was a guest or a prisoner. My hands were still tied, which had to mean something. But a bath sounded so damn good.

I took small, shuffling steps toward the staircase. It was all I could do as every muscle in my body screamed.

Noelle's face softened as I approached. "That's it. What's your name, hun?"

"Mariposa," I said in a harsh whisper.

"Okay. I know you're skittish but don't be scared, okay?"

She withdrew a knife from the sleeve of her robe, then proceeded to cut the rope binding my wrists and forearms.

"Reaper, you forgetful prick," she muttered, tossing the rope over the railing. "Men are so inconsiderate, aren't they?"

She gave me a smile, but staring back dumbly was the extent of my reaction. Inconsiderate didn't begin to cover murderer, rapist, and abuser.

"Come with me. I'll run you a bath and we'll get some food in you."

I hesitated, wondering if I could make a break for it with my hands now free, but the cramps in my thighs told me I'd end up with a broken neck if I tried going down these stairs by myself. So I followed Noelle up on shaky, excruciating steps.

"I take it you're a virgin?" She flicked a light to reveal a bathroom twice the size of my room back at the service center.

"Huh?" My eyes immediately fell to the mini-fridge stocked with bottles of water and containers of sliced fruit.

"To riding motorcycles." Noelle followed my gaze and opened the fridge, holding out a water and a covered bowl of pineapple chunks. "You're walking like you've never had one of those things between your legs before."

I was too busy tearing open the bottle to respond, dumping the sweet, delicious source of life down my throat until I choked on it.

"Easy," Noelle chuckled, turning two handles on a gigantic porcelain tub. "You'll feel sick."

I emptied the bottle and helped myself to a second one, shoving down pineapple slices in between sips.

"Feeling better?" Noelle looked amused, maybe a little annoyed, but nowhere near as downright murderous as Reaper.

I nodded, my body no longer feeling as thrashed with some food and hydration.

"The water's perfect," Noelle skimmed her hand over the surface of the bathtub. "I turned the jets on, too. They'll help with the soreness you'll feel tomorrow."

"I already feel like roadkill," I muttered, running a hand through my hair. Sand and dirt felt like it caked every inch of my skin and hair. That bath water was going to turn brown the moment I stepped in.

"Ah, she speaks." Noelle smirked. "Well, get on in. I'd give you some privacy but I'm still salty about being woken up, plus the simple fact is you're a stranger in my house. So you're just going to have to deal with me."

Nudity was nothing to me, so I didn't care if she stayed. I'd seen hundreds of different bodies in all kinds of unflattering positions. I just shrugged and stripped out of my well-loved scrubs, eager to wash away the dirt and grime of the desert.

Noelle watched me passively, perched on the edge of the tub as I shed my clothing and sank into the warm water. A soft gasp escaped my mouth at the gentle, kneading pressure of the jets on my exhausted muscles. I closed my eyes and leaned my head back to rest it on the cool, porcelain tile. For the first time in hours, I allowed myself to relax. I might still get killed, but at least I got this bath first.

"So why did my brother bring you home?" Noelle's tone was curious over the soft rumbling of the jets.

"I have no idea," I kept my eyes closed as I answered her, not yet willing to face the reality of where I was. "We've barely spoken a word to each other."

"Where did he find you?"

"At a service center in Old Phoenix."

"Did he fuck you?"

"No." I lifted my head and opened my eyes to look at her. "I don't deal in sex. I'm a trained medic. I had just gotten to that center myself and was helping in the kitchen, too. That's how I had the pleasure of meeting him." I couldn't keep the disdain out of my voice.

Noelle's tattooed eyebrows lifted as she leaned back, her face softening like my admission made perfect sense.

"I see. That explains a lot," she mused.

"I'm glad it does to you. Why not explain it to me since I'm still in the fucking dark?"

She chewed her lips slowly, now taking apparent care to watch what she said.

"Reaper and I lost someone very dear to us," she said softly. "The whole club did, really. That person would still be alive if they had gotten medical attention in time."

"So, what? I'm the new walking, talking first aid kit?" I demanded. "I can refuse to treat people, you know. You can't force me to perform my services."

"Yeah? " Noelle arched a brow with an amused smile. "You'd let people with treatable conditions just get worse and die? Somehow I doubt that, miss medic."

"He could have just asked me!" My anger was returning along with my strength. "He didn't have to kill two people, tie me up, and throw me on the back of a bike like a fucking pirate!"

"But we *are* pirates," Noelle grinned. "We don't ask, we take. It's our way of life."

"I'm a person. You can't just force me to do something against my will."

"Here's where you're forgetting something, Mariposa." Noelle leaned over the tub, bringing her face closer to mine. "There was a little event that happened six years ago called the Collapse."

"I know—"

"No, you really don't," she cut me off. "You were lucky. You were privileged enough to get your fancy medic training, but most of us weren't. So let me spell this out for you."

She grabbed my chin, forcing me to look at her.

"No one has rights anymore. Not to their body, their skills, nothing. If you want to be treated like a person, you have to fight for that. If you don't want to be forced into something, you gotta be stronger than the ones forcing you. Do you understand? Most of the time, it's easier just to go along without a fight. If you value your life, that's what I suggest you do."

She pulled back, pinning me with a green-eyed stare. "If I'm being honest, you're lucky you got picked up by my brother's crew over someone else's."

"What makes you say that?"

"Because in times like these," she rose to her feet, "things can't get much better. But they can always be much, much worse."

EIGHT

GUNNER

I drained the rest of my coffee and brought the cup down heavily on the table. Six hours of sleep after riding all night was nowhere near enough. Jandro yawned next to me in agreement. The others around the table looked just as worse for wear, but they knew better than to skip official SDMC meetings, otherwise known as church.

Only Reaper and Shadow looked bright-eyed and bushy-tailed, as far as those two scowling bastards could anyway.

"If you're all done nodding off at my table," Reaper growled. "We can begin the meeting." He struck his gavel down on the block and brought up the first and most pressing order of business.

"We will no longer be utilizing the service center outside of Old Phoenix, due to the owner being unable to keep his fucking mouth shut. We'll need a new place to stop for R&R on our eastbound ride. Any ideas?"

"How about that place that used to be a casino?"

Brick suggested, scratching his crotch. I told him not to fuck that girl or he'd catch something. "It's a bit north but not too far out of the way."

"Too big," Reaper shook his head. "With so many drifters congregating in one place, it'd be easy for someone to sneak up and gank one of us."

"You saying we need somewhere more intimate?" Jandro asked with a lazy smile. "Some place cozy and comfortable, with some home cookin'?"

Reaper rolled his eyes at his VP's choice of words, but nodded. "It was unfortunate Tom had to break our agreement, but that place was damn near perfect for our needs. Good food, space for the bikes, comfortable beds, and right on our main route. It'll be hard to replace."

"Pussy was top-notch, too," added Big G with a sad shake of his head.

Jandro shifted uncomfortably in his seat, illustrating how we all felt. Big G's wife was heavily pregnant with their third child. None of us ordinarily cared how others conducted their personal lives—we all came from different backgrounds after all. Being married with side chicks was just how some men lived their lives. But Tess was a good, loyal woman. One of the few who would never even look at another man. The least he could do was be more discreet about messing around on her.

I cleared my throat to break up the awkwardness. "Maybe we ought to look at some maps and scout some places out first. We got two weeks until our next drop, so that should give us time."

Reaper nodded. "You, me, and Jandro will discuss it

this evening at my house, if nobody else has any bright ideas."

Reaper's eyes swept across the faces at the table. When no one responded, he leaned back in his leather chair and lifted his chin at me.

"Gunner, what's the latest on this drop?"

"Smooth sailing as usual, boys," I announced, unfolding my inventory sheet with a smile to my brothers. "General Tash's resistance has the weapons they need to maintain control of the border. In exchange for ten handguns, twenty-four hunting rifles, six assault rifles, four cases of grenades, plus accessories like extended mags, scopes, and speedloaders, we have received one full pallet of the finest motor oil, already processed, half a pallet of fresh steaks, none of that dried meat, boys!"

I paused in my report to let everyone moan and salivate, rubbing their bellies at the thought of a freshly grilled hunk of meat fit for a king. Salami and jerky could only whet a man's appetite so much.

"God, I can't wait to fire up the grill tonight," Jandro licked his lips.

"We also received," I continued, "two kilos of solid copper, one kilo of high-grade steel, and one pound of dried chilis." I set my paper down. "To season our meat with, I'm assuming."

That got a light chuckle out of some people, but Reaper's voice barked out from across the table. "What's General Tash renaming the New Mexico territory again?"

"New Ireland," I scoffed with an eye roll. "Because

dried chilis and Southwestern desert is exactly what one pictures when you think of Ireland."

"So what's in store for the next drop?" Hades' black nose peered over the edge of the table next to his master, earning an affectionate ear stroke.

"Mostly ammo for the guns," I answered. "I already contacted our supplier to put that together. General Tash also asked me," I rubbed my chin, the five o'clock shadow itching my usually clean-shaven face, "about getting a few drones, which I haven't dealt with before. I'm putting some feelers out there to see what I can find but no major bites yet."

"Drones," Jandro scoffed. "Good for dropping off packages, pretty useless for actual warfare, unless anyone can break into the old Pentagon."

"Not to mention, they're easy to shoot," Reaper added. "Probably expensive and not really worth it."

"If they have cameras, the video can be saved immediately," I pointed out. "Even if the drone is lost, they're good for gathering intel. I made no promises, except to look into it."

Reaper spread his hands and shrugged. "I'm open to it, as long as the cost is low and we exchange for resources valuable to us."

"Oh, you know me, Mr. President," I winked across the table. "I'll find the best deal I can and nothing else."

"Great. So does anyone else have club business they need to address?"

Nothing but silence around the table, to which Reaper nodded. "Good. Church will resume on Sunday next week, usual time." He lifted the gavel, but before he could strike it down, Jandro raised a hand.

"Hold up, boss. You're not gonna say a word about *Marrriposa?*"

Reaper's hard scowl across the table at his VP could make a man shit himself. It only made Jandro smile smugly in return.

"We took a girl from the Old Phoenix center," Reaper voiced reluctantly. "She's currently in one of my guest rooms, and may or may not fit in to club life. That has yet to be seen."

"Pres, I've never seen you take a girl for yourself before. Why's this one special?" Big G shot him a toothy smile. "And are ya up for sharing?"

"You'll keep your cock zipped up, G," Reaper snarled at him. "The truth is, she's a medic, but that means nothing at this point. Like I said, we'll see if she fits in."

"And if she doesn't?"

Reaper lifted his eerily bright green eyes to me. "Then we'll return her to where we found her."

NINE

MARIPOSA

I had no idea how long I slept. All I knew was this bed was *damn* comfortable.

With a groan, I flopped over, pressing my face into the pillow that perfectly supported my sore neck and shoulders all night. Or all day, rather.

Sunlight peeked through thick curtains and the room was quiet. It even felt peaceful. I couldn't remember the last time I slept that deeply. Traveling on my own kept me on edge. Peace and comfort felt strange and unfamiliar.

I sat up and looked around the simply furnished room. There wasn't much to it besides the bed, a desk, dresser, and an armchair in the corner. Compared to the service station, though, it was downright luxurious.

A set of folded clothes, which I assumed to be Noelle's, sat on top of the dresser. I climbed out of bed and went to get dressed, the strangeness of this room and everything that happened crawling over me like fingers on my skin.

Why was she lending me clothes? Why was this room so nice? This was some kind of biker gang compound. Why wasn't I chained up in a dark, dingy basement?

The questions continued racing through my brain as I pulled on the breezy harem pants and form-fitting tank top. Typical desert dweller clothes, nothing that would suggest I was a prisoner.

Tiptoeing to the bedroom door, I pushed it open with painstaking care to not make a sound. Male voices floated up to my ears from somewhere downstairs. I looked both ways down the hall and saw no sign of Noelle.

I crept toward the balcony overlooking the first floor. A quick peek down showed no one near the stairs, so I began my slow descent down.

The voices grew louder and more clear as I reached the bottom, coming from somewhere near the kitchen.

"...the Sandia Mountains? It's too far out of the way, it'll be murder on the bikes..." That sounded like Jandro.

I glued myself to the wall like a gecko as I made my way closer. If they were planning a ride, maybe I could overhear when and make my escape.

"Horus can scout for us from those high vantage points. Isn't that right, boy?"

A screech echoing off the wall announced Gunner's presence with his falcon. The skin on my neck shivered at the memory of the blonde man's lips touching me, but I couldn't place if the reaction was out of disgust or enjoyment.

He associates with a murderer, I reminded myself. *And as a 2A advocate, he's very likely a murderer himself.*

"We've got to stay out of Razor Wire territory." The gruffest voice in the room could only be Reaper. "The mountains can give us shelter if we pack accordingly."

"It's a risk, man." Jandro seemed to be the only one hesitant about the idea. "It's a longer ride, big elevation climbs, plus we're going to be carrying heavier loads. Some of the older bikes might not be able to handle it."

"I'm leaving it up to you to ensure the bikes are in the best possible shape. Even if that means scrapping the old ones and putting together new ones."

"Man, you know how attached these guys are to their babies. I can't just—"

"You will."

"So, what, this is a done deal already? Don't we need to vote on this at church?"

I couldn't hear Reaper's answer over the clicking of claws on the tiled floor, growing louder with every second. When a long snout and shiny black eyes came around the corner to greet me, I panicked.

"Shoo!" I whispered at Hades, flinging my hands at him. "Go away!"

The large dog smiled at me instead, wagging his stubby tail as he lifted his front paws to my shoulders to greet me.

"Hades, no!" I groaned under his weight as I tried to shove him off. The damn dog had to weigh at least a hundred pounds and was built out of dense, solid muscle. It was like trying to shove off a person-sized brick that fell on me.

"Hades!" Reaper's voice barked from inside the dining room, followed by a high-pitched whistle.

With a soft, whining growl, the Doberman brought all four paws back to the floor but it was too late then. Heavy footsteps stomped across the floor until I was looking at three distinct but ridiculously handsome faces.

"*Marrriposa*," Jandro grinned, saying my name in that stupidly hot accent of his. "You look well-rested. And if I may say, *well*." His eyes lowered deliberately from my face to the deep V in my tank top. I felt the red flush creeping up my neck immediately.

"What were you doing out here?" Reaper was clearly not amused like his VP, but he asked the question with a simmering calm. "Eavesdropping?"

"What else am I supposed to do?" I shot back. "I'm here against my will, I have this whole house to roam, and no fucking clue why I'm here."

It was probably unwise to talk back to a killer, but not knowing a damn thing was eating away at me. I was also banking on the idea that if I was a guest in his house, my head was probably not on the chopping block. Plus his dog liked me, so that had to be something, right?

"Mm." Gunner sucked his bottom lip between his teeth, blue eyes shimmering with mischief. "She's a feisty one, Reap. Whatever you plan with her, hope you keep her around."

"Get the fuck out of here," his surly president replied. "Both of you. Get shit set up for the barbecue. I'll catch you there later."

Jandro and Gunner left while snickering to each other, which made my stomach drop.

"Hades," Reaper breathed softly. "Kennel, boy."

The dog trotted off obediently back toward the study. Then it was just the Steel Demons' president staring me down in his decked-out luxury home. He had all the power here and we both knew it. I was well and truly fucked.

"What were you hoping to gain by listening to my conversation?" He started toward me, prompting me to back away.

"What do you want from me?" I stammered in return—my mind, body, and soul now in complete fight or flight mode.

Something hit my back—the bannister to the stairs. Reaper's hands shot out to grab it on either side of me, caging me in with no escape.

"Answer my question." He leaned in so close, the intensity of his eyes burning into mine. When I lowered my gaze, I got an eyeful of those full lips and the dimple in his chin I hadn't noticed before. He had shaved since coming home.

"To find out when you'd be going on another ride," I confessed. "So I could escape."

"Escape?" he barked out a laugh in my face and pulled one hand off of the railing, gesturing to the front door. "I told you this morning. You're welcome to leave whenever you'd like."

"I don't believe you," I seethed, willing my voice not to shake. "You're a murderer. You'll leave me to die."

He rolled his eyes as if dealing with a petulant

teenager. "I'm not responsible for you if you leave this place. If you die out there, it's your own fucking problem."

I noticed he made no denial to me calling him a murderer, which just scared me even more. The way his eyes started roaming over my bare shoulders and chest made me fucking paralyzed.

"I don't see you running," he mocked. "Still too sore from the ride?"

His fingers closed around my shoulders and I gasped—partially from the fear of him touching me, but also at the pressure he put on a certain point right between my shoulder and my back.

It felt...*good*.

His fingers worked in a circle, driving deep into the knot behind my shoulder. I gasped again, the massage toeing the line between pleasure and pain. A smug grin crossed his face at my reaction.

"Turn around," he instructed.

"No."

"Turn. Around."

"I don't want to—" my lip wobbled, images of Gretchen, Kitty, and all the girls standing in my line at the service center. I didn't want to join them as one of the sea of faces used by men.

"It'll feel better if I can reach your sore spots easier," Reaper said.

"You expect me to believe that's *all* you want to do?" I hissed through gritted teeth.

He merely looked annoyed. "I don't fuck women

against their will, so you can relax. It does nothing for me."

The admission was surprising but I was not about to let my guard down. "You say that like you've tried it a few times before."

"I haven't." He withdrew his hands from my shoulders, shoving them in his jeans pockets. "The thought of it doesn't even get me hard."

"Oh, how noble of you," I sneered. "You don't rape women but you still kill people. What a stand-up guy you are."

"Can you name three men who haven't killed someone since the Collapse?" he shot back. "Of course, I kill when it's necessary. But preying on women, who are naturally smaller and weaker than men? Only cowards and weaklings do that, and I have no room for them in my club."

I stared at him, genuinely surprised to hear this coming from the leader of a ruthless road crew. So many men these days believed they were entitled to everything, including a woman's body. It was the main reason our rights were stripped away in so many areas, so we couldn't fight back with the law, our education, anything.

"So you didn't kidnap me to...have your way with me?"

A lazy grin pulled at the corners of Reaper's lips. "Do you know why SDMC has the reputation that it does?" When I shook my head, he explained, "Because I gathered a crew of *real* men. Men of strength and integrity. We're strong because we push our limits. We seek fights that challenge us. A dog doesn't get stronger by chasing prey that's already limping."

He rubbed his palms together, tilting his head in an almost dog-like way. I could see Hades doing the exact same thing. "And as a result of that," he concluded. "Women flock to us of their own free will."

My stomach tightened with a feeling I couldn't place. He, Jandro, Gunner, and even Shadow, were gorgeous specimens. Of course they had plenty of women to choose from.

"None of that explains what you want with me," I reminded him. "Noelle said you—"

His arms shot out again, muscles flexing as he gripped the bannister on both sides of me.

"Turn around and I might tell you." His voice carried a hint of teasing, a far cry from his snapping president voice.

This time I did as he ordered, my heart crashing so hard against my ribs, I was certain he'd feel it.

After a moment of nothing, the weight of his hands came down on my shoulders with more gentleness than I expected. The moment his thumbs pressed into the aching knots in my back, another gasp escaped my mouth. This time followed by a small moan.

He didn't react to the noise, the pressure of his thumbs steadily digging into my flesh. I clamped my mouth shut in an effort to not let out any more embar-rassing noises, but I couldn't help allowing my eyelids to flutter closed.

It hurt so fucking good.

When those muscles turned to jelly, he moved onto

my arms without a word, rubbing into my triceps with painful, releasing bliss.

"Why are you doing this?" I asked as the minutes stretched on, and his skilled hands moved to the center of my back.

"Because I want to and you're letting me."

"What's the *real* answer?"

"You know," he mused, fingertips skimming across my waist. "You'd enjoy this a lot more without clothes in the way."

"Not happening," I snapped.

"Just thought I'd try," he chuckled.

Any retort I had went out the window as his hands continued working magic on my back. He stayed completely focused on the muscles and didn't try to sneak a feel anywhere else. I stayed tense and alert, just waiting for him to try something but it never came.

Just as I was about to fully let go and completely melt under his touch, the pressure of his hands lifted away.

"Have you eaten today?"

I turned to face him, still a bit on edge despite being far more relaxed than before. He stood a respectful distance away, hands shoved back in his pockets with an expectant look.

"No, I guess I haven't."

"Come to the barbecue tonight." The way he said it made it clear it was an order, not a suggestion. "Have a small taste of our life, and a plate of ribeye while you're at it."

My eyes widened. "Ribeye like the steak?" Fresh

meat, especially red meat, was incredibly expensive and hard to come by.

"No, like the ribs with eyes," he teased. "Of course the steak."

"Who'd you have to kill for that?"

"No one. This time." His green eyes danced with humor, but those words slapped me with cold, hard reality.

He was a killer. And unlike men conscripted for the border wars like my father, he was comfortable joking about killing people. It didn't haunt him like it did normal men.

If nothing else, Reaper did live up to his name.

"Get cleaned up. Noelle will loan you a hairbrush, I'm sure. We'll see you there."

Ah yes, now was the perfect time to remember I just rolled out of bed and looked like a hot mess while being sensually massaged by a murderer's hands.

"We?" I repeated. "The, uh, whole club will be there?"

"Yes." His green gaze slid away from me as he turned and began a slow walk back to his study. "But so will Noelle and the old ladies of my men. The women will make you feel safe and welcome."

I watched his back retreat and he disappeared without another word.

TEN

MARIPOSA

I stared at myself in Noelle's vanity mirror as she ran a brush through my hair, which nearly hit my waist at this point.

"You lucky bitch, I'm so jealous," Noelle mused. "I wish I had hair like yours. Mine always starts breaking off when it hits a certain length. I can't let it grow past my tits for the life of me."

"Seriously?" I looked up at her reflection. "At least your color is way more fun than mine." There was nothing special about my hair, as far as I could tell. It was just a plain, normal brown.

"Oh, please," Noelle huffed. "This shit's from a box. My natural color is a dishwater dirty blonde. At least yours has some richness to it."

"Really? I figured your hair would be dark like Reaper's."

"Nah." She sprayed some kind of fruity-smelling mist over my hair before continuing with her brushing. "Aside from our eye color, no one would know we're related. We're actually half siblings. Same mom, different dads, not that it mattered to us. Daren had a different dad, too—"

She stopped talking abruptly, her face hardening as she brushed through the last of my bedhead tangles.

"Had?" I pressed gently. "Is he the one you guys lost?"

"I shouldn't talk about it," she muttered, tidying up her products on the vanity. "Reaper gets pissed if I so much as think about him. You ready?"

Deciding not to press anymore, I returned my gaze to myself in the mirror. Noelle turned my tangled, dried-out rat's nest into soft waves cascading over my shoulders. The brown locks framing my face, I looked more like my Latino dad's side of the family. The South-western sun had darkened my skin to a medium-olive, and my now-moisturized lips were redder thanks to Noelle's tinted lip balm. Only my hazel, not quite brown, eyes alluded to something else in my ancestry.

"Yeah. Thanks, Noelle." I allowed a tiny smile at my reflection. "I look like a different person."

"I knew there was a cutie-patootie hiding under there," she grinned. "Let's go. I'm dying for a steak dinner."

Following her lead down the ridiculous staircase, which no longer made my thighs scream as badly, we went out the front door and walked across the cul-de-sac to a small path through the neighborhood.

"Where is the barbecue?" I asked her, hoping my nervousness didn't show. "At someone else's house?"

"Nah, you'll see," she answered. "There's a central

clubhouse where they hold church and any kind of parties or meetings for the whole 'hood. Did I tell you what this place is called, by the way?"

"No, what?"

She smiled at me over her shoulder. "Sheol."

"What's it mean?"

"It's an old Biblical term for the grave, or Hell. Gunner thought of it. Fitting, huh?"

"Yeah…" My enthusiasm was nowhere near the same level as hers.

I smelled the food cooking before we saw it, and my stomach rippled with a growl of hunger. Voices began floating up in the warm, early evening air, accompanied by what sounded like water splashing.

We came to a flat-roofed single-story building a few minutes later, clearly the HOA clubhouse for this ritzy community before the SDMC moved in. Noelle led me around to the back side of the building. Sure enough, there was a glittering blue pool, illuminated by lights both inside and outside of the water. People were swimming, splashing, talking, and drinking.

Noelle opened the wrought-iron gate of the surrounding fence and led me inside. Only then did I get a true sense of how many people lived here.

Two men laughing over beers tended to thick, juicy steaks sizzling on a grate over a rectangular fire pit. More people, men and women, checked over the four smaller barbecue pits near the perimeter of the patio area. A large awning from the main building hung over the grills and patio furniture scattered around, while still a safe distance from the pool. Long tables stretched in front of the couches and smaller, bistro tables were placed by lounge chairs.

At least thirty people gathered here, drinking and eating together like family. What shocked me the most was seeing that there were *actual* families. I recognized one of Reaper's men holding a toddler against his waist, his arm around a woman's shoulders as he talked to another guy. I stared openly as he kissed the woman's temple, and she beamed at him with pure love in her eyes.

I felt like my brain was broken. I found it impossible to reconcile that these men—road pirates, thieves, and murderers—had children and loved ones waiting for them at home.

"Let's sit with Tessa." Noelle broke into my thoughts and pulled me toward a heavily pregnant woman sitting on one of the couches.

"Nellie!" The woman squealed and began pushing herself but Noelle put a stop to that immediately.

"Nope! None of that, old lady! You stay right where you are."

Tessa relented, relaxing back as she held her arms out to hug Noelle. "Oh, I miss you, hun," she cooed against Noelle's bright red hair. "These kids don't give me a free minute, I tell you."

"Honey, I told you I can help with them," Noelle chastised gently before looking over at me. "Tessie, this is Mariposa. Reaper brought her from a service center on the last ride."

"Ohh welcome, sweetie! Nice to meet you!" Tessa

smiled glowingly up at me. "It's so nice to see Reaper's found someone—"

"Oh no, there's nothing between us," I interrupted her. "No offense, but I didn't exactly come here willingly."

Tessa's smile didn't falter. "Well, he must've seen something special in you, to have rescued you from your situation."

I couldn't believe my ears. Was she brainwashed by these people?

"He did *not* rescue me. He kinda—"

"Hey, let's grab a drink!" Noelle cut me off with a tense smile before pulling me over to a large tub of ice with various cans and bottles stuck inside. "Can you just cool it for a damn minute?" she hissed under her breath. "I get why you're upset, but don't take it out on my pregnant, hormonal friend."

Shit, I definitely should've known better. Picking my battles was not my strong suit.

"Sorry," I sighed, leaning over the ice tub. "What's good to drink?" Maybe a few alcoholic beverages would take the edge off. *Although another massage from Reaper wouldn't hurt.*

I shook the thought from my head just as Noelle began pointing out drinks. "The hard lemonade's pretty good. The dark bottles are malt liquor some of the guys made. Drink that at your own risk."

"Hard lemonade it is." I pulled a bottle out and twisted off the cap as we made our way back to Tessa.

"Sorry about that earlier," I forced a smile at her as I sank down next to her on the couch. "I just...didn't expect to end up here and I don't know anything about MC life."

"Aww, that's all right, sweetie," she clasped one of my hands and returned my smile. "It's a different way of life, for sure. Takes some getting used to. Life after the Collapse either swallowed men up whole, or it made them stronger. These men," she nodded out toward the barbecue pits and the pool, "they're the strong ones. But carrying all that weight on their shoulders has its consequences, too. That's why they need good women around," she added with a pat to my hand.

I drank from my bottle as I listened to her. "So, I take it you're someone's old lady?"

"Mm-hmm. That one's mine right there, with the two rugrats," she pointed to the other side of the pool, where a large, burly man held the hands of two children. "You can't have him," she added with a playful smack to my thigh.

I forced a chuckle, then swallowed my response with another pull of my lemonade. That was the guy getting his dick sucked by Kitty out in the lobby. With how dreamily Tessa looked at him with their children, I couldn't imagine she had any idea.

"What about you, Noelle?" I looked down the couch to her. "Are you with anyone?"

"Hah," she scoffed. "Even if I was, Reaper would have him dead and buried within a week. The bastard's so overprotective, he's more like a father than a brother sometimes."

"Well, that's understandable, considering what

happened to Daren," Tessa mused before her gaze snapped over to me. "Do you know about him?"

"She doesn't," Noelle snapped.

"Ah, well." Tessa smoothed her hands in her lap while I wondered why everyone was so hush-hush about this Daren person. "Reaper just wants you to have a good man," she continued to Noelle. "Once you find someone worthy of you, I'm sure he'll approve."

"Again, acting like my father," the red-haired woman grumbled.

"He has to approve every union in the club," Tessa replied as if reminding her. "That's just our way."

"You ladies ready for steak?" called one of the men at the central fire pit.

"Took y'all long enough!" Noelle jumped to her feet. "Come on, Mari. Help me make a plate for Tessa."

"Better make it two," Tessa laughed, rubbing her belly.

Noelle and I grabbed paper plates and I nearly salivated when the thick, juicy hunk of meat dropped onto it. Saving the bigger one for Tessa, we made our rounds to the smaller grills where people roasted corn, potatoes, bell peppers, and other assortments of veggies and sides. If my circumstances of being here were different, I would have been thrilled to have been invited to this block party. It felt so wholesome, warm, and pre-Collapse. It made me nostalgic for the neighborhood cookouts of my childhood. I didn't know anyone still had a community like this, much less a biker gang.

"Having fun, *Marrriposa?*"

I looked up to see Jandro's flirtatious smile as he wielded a pair of metal tongs in one hand.

"I guess you could say that."

He laughed in response. "It's okay to admit you're having a good time. We know how to party." With his tongs he picked up an ear of corn from the grill, charred to perfection and slathered in butter.

"Would you like a long, hard, succulent corn to go with your thick, juicy meat?"

"Sure." I held out my plate, keeping my face neutral at his innuendo. "I'll take another one for Tessa."

"Mm, I love it when girls double up." He placed another on my second plate. "Makes everything so much more filling, doesn't it?"

"Thanks, Jandro," I grumbled, my face on fire despite my desperate attempt to be unaffected by him.

"Sure thing. Come back to me if you need more," he winked, thoroughly enjoying my discomfort.

I turned to head back to the couches, nearly crashing into a massive, dark form.

"Oh shit, I'm sorry!"

My neck craned up to meet the one dark eye staring back at me. Shadow. I didn't know how I missed seeing him with how big he was. He apparently lived up to his name.

The big man took a seat in a lounge chair next to Jandro's, bringing a large bottle to his lips and drinking deeply. My mouth fell open at the realization he was drinking straight tequila.

"Move it, girl. I'm starving," Noelle complained from behind me.

I hurried back next to Tessa, who licked her lips at the full plate I set down in front of her.

"You are a goddamn angel," she moaned as she began carving into her steak.

The three of us didn't talk much as we stuffed our faces. Tessa mumbled to Noelle between bites about her kids and pregnancy while I took the opportunity to people-watch.

Reaper and Gunner were nowhere to be seen, which surprised me. Scanning the area, I spotted Hades reclining next to a retaining wall, chewing on a bone while Horus perched on the wall above him.

The falcon gnawed at a piece of raw meat in his talon, tearing off chunks to swallow whole while Hades looked up hopefully as if waiting for a piece to drop. When the bird finished its meal without leaving a scrap behind, he let out a series of short screeches as if he were laughing. Hades responded with a toothy smile, yipping softly in return as he stretched out along the floor.

I blinked and returned to watching the humans on the patio. Watching animals act like they were communicating was a bit too trippy for me. But if they were here, their owners had to be nearby.

My attention returned to Jandro and Shadow, lounging by the grill as they drank and the handsome Latin man served up corn. While Jandro did most of the talking to his tall, dark friend, I did spot Shadow's lips moving as well.

So he's not completely silent, I thought as I chewed my steak. *He must just be highly selective as to who he talks to.*

Keeping this in mind, my eyes drifted over the pool just as a figure lifted himself out with a powerful push of his arms.

My chewed-up steak nearly fell out of my mouth at the sight of Reaper's lean, chiseled form rising out of the water. The grinning, horned skull of the Steel Demons emblem decorated his chest, accented by flames and smoke licking across from his collarbone to just below his pecs. His abs flexed as he stepped onto the pool deck, a tiny river of water running down between the ridges of muscle before he toweled himself off.

As if that sight wasn't enough, Gunner jumped out right behind him. The blonde, blue-eyed demon looked like a surfer, but coming out of the water, he could have been Poseiden himself. His long, golden locks slicked back, his physique was leaner than Reaper's. His muscles were just as prominent, but longer and with slightly less bulk. The V in his slender hips cut deep and defined, his swim trunks hanging dangerously low.

"Still think you're not Reaper's girl?" Tessa interrupted my ogling with a playful jab to my ribs. "Mr. President sure is easy on the eyes."

"Shit, two-thirds of the men here are," Noelle laughed. "That's the real torture, Mari. Being surrounded by all this eye candy."

My eyes bounced back and forth between Reaper and Gunner accepting drinks as they toweled off, a small crowd gathering around them, and Jandro and Shadow keeping quietly to themselves across the patio.

"Tell me something," I said to no one in particular. "I thought Jandro was Reaper's VP."

"He is," Tessa confirmed.

"So why are Reaper and Gunner always together, and Jandro's always with Shadow?"

My two companions exchanged glances and I wondered if, like the Daren business, this was something I wasn't supposed to know.

"All four of them are close. Best friends, basically," Noelle said, choosing her words carefully. "But Shadow is kind of a black sheep, as you can tell."

"He's not right in the head," Tessa added in a whisper.

"Well, something happened to him," Noelle explained. "I don't know exactly but whatever it was, Jandro knows best how to deal with him."

"He's like a service dog," Tessa nodded. "A service human, I guess."

"And Gunner is the club's arms dealer and captain of the guard," Noelle said. "He's basically the one in charge of bringing in all the goods to our community, so he always has Reaper's ear."

"I see." I bit off more steak and chewed it thoughtfully.

"Jandro's a good VP," Noelle mused. "He's one of those who considers all options, while my damn brother is more of a hot head. They balance each other well. It's just Jandro's usually stuck babysitting Shadow."

I hung onto every word she said, carefully filing the information away to use later.

For when I finally could escape without losing my life.

ELEVEN

REAPER

G unner was only better than me at two things in life—negotiating weapons deals and holding his breath under water.

My lungs burning, I burst out of the water first. Again.

"Son of a bitch's tit," I muttered, pulling myself up out of the pool.

"Whooo!" the blonde asshole hollered, raising his fists as he flipped his hair back like a fucking mermaid. "I win again! I'll take my steak medium-rare, boss."

"You'll take my balls on your chin nicely, too," I shot back, snapping a towel at him with a grin. "Give me a second to dry off."

"Oh, I got all fuckin' night." He rubbed a towel over his head, making his hair stick out in all directions like a lion's mane, before grabbing a beer from an ice bucket and heading off to mingle.

After thoroughly drying my torso, I wrapped my towel around my waist and took a seat in a chair near the pool. I took a moment to soak it all in, the atmosphere and the energy. These were my people, and I was responsible for them.

Everyone seemed happy. The air felt upbeat and positive. We had a good run. Gunner negotiated a hell of a deal with General Tash and the exchange went smoothly, with both sides delivering exactly as promised. And most importantly, we didn't lose anyone.

I fished a beer out of the bucket next to me and cracked it open, taking long pulls as I people-watched. Dallas and Andrea kissed, staring at each other all googly-eyed while their kids chased each other around the fire pit. Big G played Marco Polo in the pool with his kids. Even Shadow was saying a few words, by the looks of it.

Something cold and wet nudged the edge of my palm, and I looked down to see Hades nuzzling me. I scratched his ears as he rested his head on my knee, looking up at me with those impossibly dark eyes.

"How long's it gonna last, boy?" I asked, moving the scratches down to his neck. "How long can I keep these people safe from what's out there?"

He licked my hand with a soft yip, then lifted his head from my leg to look behind him. Right at Mariposa, sitting between Noelle and Tessa.

The one place I refused to look.

With a sigh, I followed my dog's gaze. My eyes traveled up her legs, whose shape I could still make out in those loose harem pants, to the dipping curves of her waist. I was biting inside my cheek during that massage earlier, wrestling the urge to see just how well my hands would fit in those sweet curves.

As my eyes moved up, relishing in the swells of her tits and her long, graceful neck, her eyes jerked away from mine right before our gazes met. She suddenly appeared very interested in the conversation Noelle and Tessa were having.

I adjusted my dick and polished off my beer, then rose to grab a steak to throw on the grill for Gunner. As soon as the meat began sizzling, I grabbed another beer and meandered to where the women sat.

"Get enough to eat?"

Mariposa jumped at the sound of my voice. A whole lot of good that massage did, jumpy and tense as she was. Not that I would mind touching her again, preferably with less clothing on.

"Yes," she said carefully, watching me sit on the couch next to her. "And it was delicious, thank you."

"We've gone from threatening escape to thanking me," I noted. "Not bad progress for your first day here."

She bristled, her hands clenched in her lap. "I'll never be ungrateful for a good meal. No matter who it comes from."

"Splendid. You just may learn how to live in a post-Collapse society after all." I stood again to check Gunner's steak. The moment I turned my back, Hades stuck his face between her knees and turned up the puppy dog eyes.

"Why the hell does my dog like you so much?" The question had been on my mind since I watched him sit on his ass for a treat from her.

"I don't know." She massaged his face with her thumbs. "Dogs can sense things people can't. I had a veterinarian friend say they can smell your emotional state. Whether you're afraid, angry, or happy."

"Hades definitely smells fear." I flipped Gunner's steak. "But his normal reaction is to get his teeth in their face and turn that fear into terror, not ask for pets."

"Well, maybe he knows something else about me."

"Like what?"

"I'm not sure." Her eyes lifted to me again. "Maybe he knows all I try to do is help people."

"Huh," I scoffed. "Gunner! Come get your fucking steak!"

"Why, thank you, boss." His hair now fluffy like newborn chick feathers, he marched over to me with a shit-eating grin and his chest puffed out. "It better be medium-rare or you're gonna have to cook me another one."

"Don't push your luck, bimbo." I passed over the meat on a plate, noticing his eyebrows lift with curiosity at me sitting so close to Mariposa.

I ignored him and went back to sit down, her last sentence mulling around in my head.

"So if I or any of my men were badly injured," I mused, "you'd still try to save us?"

"Yes," she answered without hesitation. "It's my duty as a medic to protect life. I swore an oath upon completing nursing school."

"Huh," I scoffed again, almost choking on my beer. "Oaths are meaningless."

Her expression didn't change. "Not if you take them to heart. I've never gone against my oath to save lives."

"Really?" I leaned in closer to her. "You're telling me if Garold Richardson was lying at your feet right now, bleeding to death, you'd do everything in your power to save his life?"

Her eyes narrowed at the man's name, the eightieth and last President of the United States, and the dipshit who plunged the country headfirst into the Collapse. According to multiple radio announcements, he was one of the first to abandon this mess he created, taking off on his private jet to Morocco or who-the-fuck knows where.

"Yes," she replied with a bit more hesitation this time. "It doesn't matter who the person is. If a life is in danger, I'm sworn to save it."

"Hmm." I didn't entirely believe her. "You may be the only person in the world who takes your oath that seriously."

"It wouldn't matter if he died before, you know, all this," she continued softly. "At least I don't think so. The Collapse would have still happened whether he or some other bureaucratic shithead was in office."

"You're probably right," I mused, rubbing my jaw. "The Collapse was a long time coming."

"Seems you've done well for yourself." Her expression was somewhere between curious and challenging. My beer paused on its way to my mouth and I wasn't sure how to respond.

A smile twitched on my lips and I almost forgot about my regret of bringing an educated woman into my club. Not many people challenged me these days, and I forgot how much I liked it.

"Reaper?"

A shrill voice cut into my thoughts, quickly followed by a low warning growl from Hades.

"Heather," I returned begrudgingly to the woman making her way across the patio to me. Her bolted-on tits defied gravity in a way that I never cared for. Come to think of it, her fried, bleached blonde hair and caked-on makeup never did it for me either. Hindsight is 20/20 after all.

"You haven't come to see me since you got back," she pouted, crossing her arms under those ridiculous melons.

"I've been busy," I said dismissively. "So have you, apparently." I nodded to the two guys she'd been sucking face with all night, Bones and Python. They nodded back to me and lifted their drinks in respect.

"I'm never too busy for you, Mr. President," she cooed, running a manicured finger along my jawline. "Want to go back to your house? I missed you."

"I will eventually," I said, batting her hand away. "But not with you."

Her face fell. "Why not?"

"Because I don't want to fuck you." I shot her my best apologetic look. "It's nothing personal."

"But...why?" she asked with such a crestfallen look, as if it never occurred to her that a man could say no to sex.

"Because I'm fucking tired of questions like these," I

snarled. "Almost as tired of thrusting my dick into you while you lie back and do nothing."

Python choked on his drink and a few conversations near us went quiet. I didn't set out to humiliate her, but the woman should've known to take no for an answer, especially from her president.

"Is there someone else?" Her lip wobbled. Fuck me, she would not quit.

"Of course there is." It wasn't true, not right at that moment. But I'd have some chick worshiping my cock soon enough for that statement to be true.

"Who?" Heather demanded, her eyes falling on Mariposa, who watched the whole exchange silently. "Who the hell are *you?* I've never seen you here before!"

"Bones, Python," I snapped before Mariposa could answer. "Come get your woman under control."

Both of them jumped to attention, practically shoving each other out of the way to reach her first.

"Sorry, Reaper," Bones mumbled, a blush creeping up his bald head. "We didn't know if you'd take her up on it."

"I won't be anymore, not after this bullshit. She's all yours, boys." I turned back to Heather, holding my index finger up in her face. "You don't make demands of me. You don't beg me for shit. If I give you an answer, you take it and move on. You're not in charge of anything here, especially not my cock. You understand me, woman?"

Hades growled louder and barked, snapping his teeth near her legs for added effect.

"Yes, Reaper," she whispered meekly, shrinking back to her two men, who looked at me expectantly.

"Punish her as you see fit," I sighed, reclining on the couch. "I'm done being involved."

"Yes, Reaper." They marched her away through the gate surrounding the pool.

I drained the last of my second beer, feeling Mariposa's eyes on me the whole time.

"What are they going to do to her?" she asked.

"Don't know, don't care." I rested a hand on my chest, partially on the SDMC skull inked there. "Not my problem anymore. They're not the brightest bunch, but they won't break any club laws."

"You said punish her." Mariposa's voice was more tense than a guitar string. "What does that entail?"

I shrugged. "Spanking. Whipping. Tying her to the bed for a full day. Not letting her orgasm for a month. Giving her an embarrassing tattoo. Walking her around on a dog leash. Whatever they see fit. Nothing that causes long-lasting harm."

Her shoulders relaxed just slightly, making me remember how they melted under my touch earlier today. The thought made my fingers on my chest twitch.

"That still seems harsh." She chewed her plump lower lip. "Heather clearly has feelings for you."

"Which are not reciprocated," I retorted. "She's so desperate to be someone's old lady, she'll let any man take a ride. She only had feelings for my position as president."

"Wow, a man talking disparagingly about someone

he slept with to another woman," she sneered. "Color me *not* impressed."

I let out a dry chuckle. "Careful, Mariposa. You're in my kingdom now. I like your snark, but you don't want to see yourself on the receiving end of one of *my* punishments."

MARIPOSA

Reaper's interaction with Heather stayed on my mind all next morning, while Noelle and I helped Tessa catch up on chores at her house.

"Doesn't Big G help you around the house at all?" Noelle asked as she moved a pile of laundry.

"He's too busy being the fun parent," Tessa said with an eye roll. "Right now he's on his patrol shift around the perimeter. When he gets home, the kids are going to be all over him and all this cleaning will be for nothing."

"I don't envy you," Noelle chuckled before tossing a stuffed dog at me. "What's on your mind over there, space case?"

"Heather," I admitted, folding a freshly dried bedsheet.

"Oh, don't worry about her," Tessa sank into a beanbag chair with a groan. "I know there's 'nothing'," she air-quoted, "between you and Reaper, but she's honestly no threat to that."

"Those two guys she was with," I said. "Is that common in MCs? For men to, uh, share a woman?"

Tessa and Noelle both laughed. "You really ain't from around here," Noelle teased me gently. "You never heard of those, what do you call 'em, the societies where the women are in charge?"

"Matriarchal?"

"Yeah, that's the one! There used to be a bunch of small ones in Arizona and Utah way before the Collapse, of course. They formed like thirty years ago as a response to the government turning to shit."

"Seriously?" I gaped at her. "I had no idea."

"No one did," Tessa chimed in. "They were very secretive about it."

"Only women and children were allowed into their communities without question. Some allowed men, but had very selective criteria," Noelle continued. "Ones that were honest, would be good protectors, help raise the children, and," she smirked, "I heard some of them were tested on their bedroom skills."

"I would've loved to be on the judge's panel for oral skills," Tessa sighed. "I love a man who knows how to use his tongue."

"A good tonguing is nice, but I'll take a thick cock on the hour, every hour," Noelle grinned. "Doesn't have to be an anaconda, just good and girthy."

"I used to feel the same way, until I ended up pregnant three times," Tessa lamented. "Being addicted to thick dick has grave consequences."

The two of them howled with laughter while I openly stared. Even in nursing school, while discussing and being surrounded by body parts all the time, I never heard anyone talk like this.

"You're gonna wake up the kids," Tessa squealed, wiping tears from her eyes.

"So the women in these societies," I said when they calmed down. "They had multiple male partners?"

"Oh, yeah. It sounds weird but it was one way they kept the power in their hands," Noelle said.

"How?"

"It was like," she thought for a moment. "Like it showed how sacred and necessary we are. How much power our bodies have. Creating life being just one of those things." She patted Tessa's belly affectionately. "The whole movement of those societies was like a protest to society at large trying to take our power away. Powerful men always surround themselves with women, so why can't we do the same thing? Kind of like that."

"How do you know so much?" I asked her.

Her expression and body language stiffened, losing all the humor from moments before.

"My ma was in a matriarchal group." She busied herself with sorting more laundry.

I remembered when she mentioned having a different dad from Reaper and her other brother. It never occurred to me that her mom may have been with them all at the same time.

The air in the room shifted just after Noelle spoke. She busied her hands and made no eye contact. Tessa stared at her with a look of sympathy.

"I'm sorry," I said. "I didn't mean to bring up something painful for you."

"It's all right," Noelle shot me a smile. "Anyway, you were asking about Heather. I don't know her but it's possible she was born in one of those groups, too. But between us? She's just desperate for dick."

"Your brother's dick in particular," Tessa agreed.

"She just wants to prance around as the president's old lady," Noelle scoffed. "Snakey bitch acted like she wanted to be my friend just to get closer to him. I saw right through that shit."

"You gonna throw a punch at her at Fight Night?"

"Hell, maybe I will!"

"What's Fight Night?" I asked, a tremor of nervousness already creeping into my voice.

"Ohh shit, she doesn't know about that either!" Tessa squcaled with delight. "You're in for a treat, Mari!"

"Basically the whole club gathers in front of our house to watch two people fight," Noelle explained. "We do it once a month just to let off some steam, settle any ongoing arguments between people. Gunner's men watch closely and call fights before it gets lethal."

"So it's like *Fight Club*?"

"You mean that movie from like a hundred years ago?" Tessa's eyes brightened. "Yes! Just like that. Only we're allowed to talk about it and girls can fight, too."

"Can I punch Reaper?" I asked, only half-jokingly.

"Nope," Noelle laughed. "Trust me, I want to hit him too sometimes. But at Fight Night, girls can only fight other girls. You can't have weapons on you, and that includes long nails. I think that's all the rules."

"You forgot the last one," Tessa piped up. "If you get challenged, you're not allowed to back down."

"That's right. And you're exempt 'cause of that kid inside you."

"Yeah. I kind of wish I could fight," Tessa sighed, running a hand along her abdomen. "I threw down on some bitches back in my day." She shot me a wink. "What do you say, Mari? Gonna get in the ring tonight?"

"No way," I shook my head. "I'm a healer, not a hitter."

———

I COULD FEEL the aggression in the air the moment Noelle and I stepped outside. A crowd had already gathered in the cul-de-sac in front of Reaper's house. That dog barking its head off had to be Hades.

The night had cooled off considerably, a small bit of relief to the heat of bodies pressing close together. I hadn't seen Reaper all day, considering I spent it with the women but there he stood at the far end of the circle forming in the cul-de-sac. A king with no throne. Or rather, the only throne he sat in was his bike seat.

He wore faded black jeans, motorcycle boots, and no shirt under his leather cut. The SDMC skull on his chest peeked through, the PRESIDENT patch and reaper scythe on his left side the only non-black part of his getup.

Two men on motorcycles rode around in figure-eight patterns, revving up their engines and pumping their fists in the air. They drummed up the crowd, feeding their bloodlust with the roars of their machines.

Jandro was the first to step into the circle, peeling off his cut and tossing it to someone in the crowd. Forgetting myself, I stared thirstily as he swaggered back and forth in search of an opponent.

He was the shortest and stockiest of Reaper's men, but still a full head taller than me and built like a brick house. He flexed those thick arms and people cheered—mostly women. As he turned around, I spotted the SDMC skull tattooed on his ribs, along with a portrait of a woman on the other side. I didn't get a close look, but she had colorful face paint in the style of Day of the Dead skulls.

I was too busy staring at the muscles upon muscles of Jandro's back, his arms, and his chest, that I didn't notice him stopping right in front of me until he spoke.

"*Marrriposa*," he grinned, moving closer until he stood directly in front of me. "How about a *besito* for good luck?"

Jesus. Why did he smell so good?

"No."

His hazel eyes widened for the full puppy-dog effect as he pointed to his cheekbone.

"Not even just a little one?"

I didn't want to open that door of intimate contact, not even a crack. Reaper's massage had already been too much. I'd been craving his hands on me all day, even though I was barely sore anymore. I hated the feeling of wanting anything from these men.

But I also knew Jandro wouldn't go away until he got something.

So I leaned in, reaching on my tiptoes, and brushed a soft kiss against his cheek.

His arm locked around my waist the moment my lips touched him, pinning me to his bare chest with the strength of an ox.

And goddamnit, he felt so warm and his skin was surprisingly soft.

Then I felt his lips on my neck, the exposed side from my leaning in to kiss him, and the gentle suction followed by a flick of his tongue.

It was over before I realized what had happened. He released me, walking backward into the circle with that infuriating grin by the time my brain caught up to what he did.

My hand slapped to my neck, my pulse racing. *That motherfucker.* My skin was still wet from his tongue. *Oh, Christ. Did he give me a hickey?*

I felt hot enough to burst into flames. I could still feel the pressure of his arm braced against my lower back, the beating of his heart against mine.

My eyes remained glued to him as he looked over the crowd, his panty-melting smile now turned predatory.

Suddenly, I really wanted to see him fight.

"Do I have any volunteers?" His voice rose crisply into the night sky, hands spread out to his sides. "Whoever's wanted to land one on your vice president, now's your chance!"

Soft murmurs traveled through the crowd, but no one seemed eager to jump in the ring with him.

"Anyone?" he taunted, licking his lips. "I'll even let you take the first swing!" When no one stepped up, he shook his head as if disappointed. "All right, then I'm picking—"

"Me!"

Everyone turned to look at a guy in his early twenties with a similar height and build as Jandro, but not nearly as muscular. He didn't look terribly confident in himself, but seemed determined. Like the other club members, he too wore a cut, but his didn't have any patches.

"Prospect," Jandro purred delightedly, beckoning the young man forward. "Come here."

The guy swallowed and clenched his fists at his sides as he stepped into the circle.

"What makes you want to fight me tonight, Prospect?" Jandro asked innocently.

The guy swallowed again and took a deep breath. "For that thing you did in the shop."

"And that was?" Jandro pressed. "Let it out, kid. This is the night to get all that shit off your chest."

"When you...you..." He sucked in a deep breath and tried again. "When you shoved my head in that bucket of dirty oil."

The crowd burst into uproarious laughter. Even Reaper covered his mouth and chuckled. But I could only stare in open-mouthed shock.

"It's what you signed up for, Prospect," Jandro replied with a shrug. "But I get it. You're tired of being pushed around and you wanna hit back. So come on, boy." He beckoned him closer with his fingers. "Like I said, I'll let you take the first swing."

The young man stepped closer, sweat already forming on his brow. He shrugged off his cut, leaving it on the ground behind him. No one held onto it for him. He approached Jandro cautiously, their eyes glued to each other.

I could already tell there was no way this kid would win. The difference between his and Jandro's movements were like a sea lion approaching a bull. He'd be lucky to land anything on the vice president.

They circled each other for what felt like a full minute before the prospect took his swing. He aimed for Jandro's head, but was slow and unbalanced, leaning too much of his weight into the punch. The VP dodged it easily, his hands still relaxed at his sides. The return strike came almost too fast to be seen. The prospect's head snapped to the side and he stumbled, spitting blood on the pavement.

I wanted to cover my eyes but couldn't look away. The crowd cheered at the violence and bloodshed, but I could barely stand it. My job was to put people back together. Why would they hurt each other intentionally?

Jandro at least waited until the prospect was steady on his feet again. His next punch came to the man's belly, making him double over. Jandro then grabbed the back of his opponent's neck and drove a knee into his ribs. The prospect crumpled to the ground and raised one shaky hand.

"Stop...no more," he wheezed.

Cheers broke out and Jandro lifted his fists victoriously to the sky. He winked at me and bit his lip suggestively, but I was too stunned to respond.

In the next moment, he leaned over to say something into the defeated man's ear and patted his back encouragingly. To my utter shock, he held out a hand and lifted him to his feet. Together, the two men walked through the crowd of people to the sidewalk in front of Reaper's house, where Jandro sat him down and shoved a beer in his hand before returning to everyone else.

Knowing I couldn't just stand by and do nothing, I approached Jandro's defeated opponent once he was left alone.

"Hi," I said, kneeling in front of him. "I'm a medic. Will you allow me to look over your injuries?"

"Um." He looked up at me nervously, blood still dripping from his mouth. "I don't think Reaper will like—"

"Reaper doesn't control what I do," I cut him off. "I'm asking *you*. Would you like my help or not?"

"Um, okay."

I moved closer, inspecting his lip as closely as I could in the dim streetlight.

"I'm Mariposa. What's your name?"

"Stephan," he answered. "But just call me Prospect."

"Why? What does that mean?" The bleeding from his mouth had slowed, which meant he hadn't lost a tooth or part of his tongue. I moved on to ribs.

"It means I'm like an apprentice," he explained. "I'm not an official member of the club until I prove myself. So I don't have any patches on my cut and I do everyone's dirty work." He turned his head to the side and spit out a mouthful of blood before taking a long pull of beer.

"And what, you just have to put up with them abusing you?"

"It's hazing," he corrected me gently. "And yeah, it's just part of it, like Jandro said. He didn't even let me work in the shop with him until last month."

"So he gives you the privilege of a skilled job, then dunks your head in dirty oil?" I shook my head in disbelief. "How long have you been a prospect?"

"About six months. I hope to be patched in by a year." His eyes brightened. "Jandro told me I did good today. That stepping up for Fight Night earned me a lot of respect."

"I don't understand it," I sighed, pulling my hands back. "But he didn't injure you too badly, thankfully."

"Oh, I knew he wouldn't. It doesn't even hurt, really."

"That's the adrenaline talking," I chuckled. "You're going to be sore as hell tomorrow, though."

"Worth it." He gave a smile, which would have been cute if his teeth weren't smeared in blood. "Hey, can you do me a quick favor?"

"Sure."

"Can you grab my cut for me? I should be wearing it."

"All right." I rose to my feet, turning back to the circle of people getting hyped up for the next fight.

"And, uh, thanks," he called after me shyly. "For checking me over. Real nice of you."

"Just doing my job."

I slithered my way between bodies, already slick with sweat. Keeping my eyes on the ground in search of the patchless cut, I paid no mind to whoever stood in the circle. Not until I was called.

"Hey! New bitch on the block!"

I looked up, dread filling the pit of my stomach.

Heather stood in the middle of the circle, black combat boots on her feet, ripped black tights adorning her legs under a pair of black booty shorts. A white crop top showed off a stomach much leaner and flatter than mine.

Dark, smoky shadow surrounding her glaring eyes, and her bleached hair pulled back in a high ponytail completed her look.

"You looking for this?" She held up the blank leather cut with a cruel smile. "Fight me for it."

THIRTEEN

MARIPOSA

"**I**'m not fighting you."

"Oh, yes you are." Heather's smile twisted into a hard grimace. "You came out here so I assume you know the rules. I challenged you, now you can't back out like a pussy."

"I'm not even part of this club!" I yelled back, panic rising within me as I searched the crowd for sympathetic faces. Someone, anyone, who'd be on my side in this.

"Neither is the prospect, not yet anyway." Heather smugly pointed out the flaw in my logic. "Nor am I. I'm just fucking two of them."

Any fleeting hope I had to escape this fight began to disappear. Reaper watched us both with passive curiosity, like this was some spectator sport on TV. Gunner, Jandro, and even Shadow looked on with bright eyes, eager for the action to start. Only Noelle had the decency to look worried, mouthing *sorry*, when her eyes caught mine.

Fuck, fuck, fuck. There was really no getting out of

this for me, was there? I'd never even thrown a punch at someone before. I couldn't go toe-to-toe in a fight with an old man in a nursing home, let alone a scrappy mean bitch like this.

"Heather," Reaper barked, his voice cutting through the air.

All heads turned to him. Sitting on the ground in front of him, Hades' ears were pinned back but the dog was silent.

"Yes, baby?" Heather asked sweetly, twirling the end of her ponytail in her hand as she turned to face him.

"Got steel toes in those boots?"

"Nope." She tapped one toe on the ground and my stomach dropped. Fuck, I didn't even think about that. "Want to check 'em?"

"Nah. Carry on." Reaper returned to his original stance with arms crossed, waiting for the action to begin.

Someone pushed me forward and I went stumbling into the circle, not even six feet away from Heather. All I had on were a pair of Noelle's sandals, my freshly cleaned scrub pants, and another borrowed tank top. A fight was the last thing I was ready for, and Heather knew it.

All I could hope was for someone to stop it before I died. I still had to get the fuck out of this place.

Heather grinned maniacally as we made a slow circle around each other, just as Jandro and Prospect did. *You'll survive*, I told myself. *You'll survive.*

She lunged, heading straight for my middle to tackle me to the ground. My panic froze me and I did nothing but scream in pain as my back hit pavement. It spread all the way to my limbs, which I couldn't even bring up to defend myself. Fuck, a back injury could really screw me.

She grabbed a fistful of my hair and started with the punching. One, two, three, times across my face. My head bounced off the ground with each blow. *Yeah, a concussion wouldn't be so great, either.*

My ears rang and a mixture of blackness and stars dotted my vision. I heard distant yelling but couldn't make any of it out. I was so disassociated from what was happening, I forgot there was a crowd of people watching, probably urging this bitch to kill me.

Come on, Wilder. You know body parts. What does she have exposed? What's vulnerable?

I could barely see through my eyes now swelling shut. My face felt wet and I tasted a big mouthful of blood, but from the weight I felt, my adrenaline-stricken mind gathered she was straddling me. So I drove a knee up, just hoping to take her by surprise and buy an extra second, maybe two.

And it fucking worked.

My knee hit her somewhere in the back or the butt, I wasn't sure. But it made her fall forward. Through my bloody, blurred vision I knew she was close enough to my face to kiss me. So I grabbed her by the throat and squeezed.

Heather let out a gurgle of surprise then immediately started thrashing, clawing and twisting to get my hand off, but I held on like my life depended on it.

I used my free hand to punch her in the stomach, probably weak as hell but what else could I do?

At some point I couldn't hold any longer and she broke away, coughing and gasping for air. Somehow I got my feet underneath me, the ground rolling as if threatening to bring me down again. Heather was doubled over, coughing and trying to suck in big gulps of air. I stumbled over to her as she tried to get away, and just as I fell, I brought an elbow down right on top of her kidneys.

I couldn't tell if that ear-shattering scream was hers or mine, but I felt a hard kick to my ribs and the bite of the pavement on my face. There she was again, a face floating among the stars and blurred colors of my vision, so I swung my fist and hit something.

I felt wetness on my knuckles, and bones underneath soft skin, so I hit again and again, no longer certain where I was or what I hit.

At some point, my fist swung and hit nothing. Someone grabbed me from behind, so I twisted and tried to kick, but a voice came through the ringing.

"Stop, Mariposa. It's over."

"No! The fight's not over!"

"It should have ended minutes ago!" snarled whoever held me. "Get the fuck out of my way!"

Was that...*Reaper?*

The world spun and I thought was falling again, but no ground slammed up to hit me. As the voices and commotion drifted away, I realized somewhere in my foggy brain that I was being carried.

"What're you..." I squirmed in vain to get away from this person holding me under the knees and across my back in a bridal position.

"Stop it. I'm helping you."

That gruff voice was so close and clear now, I froze in disbelief. I almost felt Reaper's lips brush across my forehead as he spoke. This had to be a dream, or a hallucination. I definitely had a concussion. But then I heard his voice again.

"I want to show you something."

Oh, fuck. He's gonna feed me to his pack of dogs. That's why he kept me and fed me well at the barbecue last night. I'm dog food.

Wetness caressed the fingers of my hand hanging down. I thought it was blood so I tried to flick it away, only to feel a cold nose and a gentle tongue licking me again.

Hades. It felt like he was reassuring me that I was safe. I hoped he was right. Everything hurt and I couldn't fight anymore. And I was so fucking tired of trying to protect myself.

Succumbing to my exhaustion, I allowed my head to drop onto Reaper's shoulder. It was a good, solid shoulder.

I didn't know how long he carried me for, but his strength never faltered. At some point I heard a click and a door open, then bright lights stabbed me like knives in the eyeballs.

"Ahh!" I ended up burying my face more in Reaper's shoulder, practically nuzzling him.

"Sorry. When your eyes adjust, let me know what you think."

He sat me down on a cold, flat surface, then the support and heat of his body was gone. I brought my hands to my face, partially to check my injuries but also to shield my eyes, which now felt incredibly light-sensitive.

Some cursory poking and prodding of myself told me I didn't break any bones in my face. I probably looked like a bruised, half-rotten tomato, though. Blinking carefully, I slowly lowered my hands to gaze at what Reaper wanted to show me.

"What...is this?" I breathed in disbelief.

"The medic's office," he said, opening a drawer and pulling out a washcloth. He wet it under the sink and wrung it out before approaching me slowly. I sat frozen as he gently touched the cool, wet cloth to my cheek. Nothing ever felt so good in my life. He hesitated for only a moment before dabbing away at the blood on my face. I decided to distract myself from the swirling confusion at the gentle way he touched me, plus the fact he was caring for me at all, by looking around the room.

It looked exactly like a pre-Collapse doctor's office. Reaper sat me on the counter, but there was a bed complete with the sheet of paper covering it. The cabinets held tongue depressors, cotton balls, gloves, syringes with various sizes of needles, first aid supplies, surgical sutures and more. As my eyes moved along the lower cabinets, I also spied rows of pills. My vision was too fucked to make them out, but I could only imagine they were likely pain medications and antibiotics. Some of the hardest and most expensive drugs to come by.

"Where did you get all this?" I asked Reaper.

"Gunner," he answered simply, dropping the now blood-soaked washcloth into the metal trash can. He pulled open another drawer to reveal a box of sealed alcohol wipes. Grabbing a handful, he tore open one and began cleaning the cuts on my face.

"So Gunner's a skilled procurer of weapons *and* medical supplies?" I couldn't look at his eyes as he examined and touched me. It was too intense. He was so close. And like Jandro, he smelled really fucking good.

"No," he chuckled. "This was a nurse's office before we took over the community. It had already been raided by the time we showed up, of course. But an inventory list was taped to the wall. I told Gunner to get everything on it and then some. He's the best at what he does, so he made it happen."

"And why would you want a nurse, ah, medic's office?"

"Isn't it obvious?" He pulled away from me, those green eyes still every bit as intense. "Our way of life is dangerous. I trust my men with my life, but not everyone gets that privilege. Therefore, my men are not easily replaceable. I need to be able to keep them alive."

"So all you need's someone with the skills to do it," I concluded. "That's why you kidnapped me. And yet you let me get my ass beat."

"I can't interfere with Fight Nights. It's club law, which I am not above," he said. "Tell you what. I'll teach you a few things. So you can get her back next month and you'll be even."

"That's a shitty apology," I spat out. "And I'm sure you'll go back to fucking her anyway."

I had no idea where that last outburst came from. It sounded jealous and petty. My brain had been knocked around in my skull too many times, that had to be it. In any case, it was too late to take it back.

Reaper only grinned as he closed the distance between us again. He wedged open my thighs to stand between them, hands anchored on my hips and his chest just skimming contact with mine.

"How's this for an apology?" he whispered before cupping the back of my head and slanting his lips over mine.

My poor, rattled body exploded with new sensations. Shock, warmth, fear, and *what the fuck, he's a damn good kisser.*

As if by instinct, my mouth parted for his, letting his tongue slip through. When I realized I could still taste blood, I tried to pull away, but he held strong onto the back of my head and shoved his tongue in deeper, as if he *liked* the taste of my blood.

Every kiss rolled seamlessly into another, like he was savoring me. The blood rushing to my lips couldn't have been good for my open wounds, but his mouth was like a soothing balm over mine.

I didn't know how much I needed this, not until my sore, scraped hands reached up to wrap around his neck, my fingers threading through his rich, dark hair to deepen the kiss.

When my last touch was violent, I needed this to feel better. When my last kiss was in a drunken, sloppy haze over a year ago, I needed a skilled mouth like his to remind me of how good it could be.

The moment he pulled away for a breath, insecurities hit me like another punch to the face. After what just happened, how kissable did I really look? I sure as shit didn't even win that fight. Why wasn't he kissing and fucking Heather, who was surely riding high on beating me into the pavement?

His gaze had softened, eyes hooded with lust and taking off the edge of that intensity. He kissed my forehead and my swollen, bruised eyes. It almost seemed like he was reassuring me.

"You fought well," he murmured, lips grazing my cheekbone. "With some training, you can hold your own against anyone."

"I'm not a fighter," I protested, hyperaware of his hands returning to my waist. They felt so good massaging me, now his kisses seemed to be soothing my pains as well. What kind of witchcraft was this?

"Oh? You're a lover, then?"

I didn't miss the implication in his tone, nor the way his arms circled around me or how his lips found their way to my neck. Heather hadn't touched me there, only Jandro did.

A strange rush of heat filled me at the thought of two men kissing me in the same place less than an hour apart.

"I'm a healer," I answered. "And if I have to go along with your violent traditions, I won't be able to do my job."

"Let's make a deal then." Reaper paused to kiss my bare shoulder before lifting his face to mine again. "You'll be exempt from Fight Nights if you agree to be my club's medic."

I didn't know if I wanted to hit him or kiss him

again.

"You know I can't refuse that," I seethed through my teeth. "Because of what I told you last night. Not much of a deal, is it?"

He lifted one broad shoulder in a lazy shrug. "I wanted to learn more about you before offering you anything. A medic that leaves my men to die isn't of much use to me."

I stared at him. "Were you waiting to see if I would help the people who fought tonight?"

He dipped his head in a small nod. "I value people who are true to their word. I wanted to see if you were true to yours."

"And Heather?"

"I've never seen her fight before. I didn't expect her to jump in, much less challenge you."

"And if she finds out about us...doing this?" He looked amused at my awkward gesturing between us. "You think she's going to wait until Fight Night to jump me again?"

"Yes," he insisted. "Fight Night is the only way she can take her feelings out on you and remain in the club. She won't try to subvert my authority."

"And your authority says what exactly?"

"That if she harms another club member, she'll be lucky to leave here with her life." He leaned in close again, his breath fanning over my aching lips. "Also that I'm not hers and I can kiss, touch, and fuck whomever I damn well please."

He rolled his hips between my thighs, just enough for me to feel his hardness pressing through his jeans.

Sweet Jesus, the last time I felt a man inside me was before the Collapse. Nursing school kept me too busy for a relationship and I wasn't a casual sex kind of girl. And after school? Well, I didn't have the best opinion of men. Especially not this one pressing himself between my legs, no matter how well he kissed or likely fucked.

"Why are you protecting me?" I asked.

"Because you've proved yourself to be honest. And you're useful to me." His hands traveled up my sides. "And if you want something that's reasonable, just let me or Gunner know. I'm sure we can be useful to you, too."

A shiver went down my spine at all the things that word could mean. Useful for what? For feeling kisses like these? More massages? Or just…more?

"I don't understand." My brain felt like it was desperately trying to stay above water. "Why me? Why not anyone else from the service center?"

"You were the only medic, of course," Reaper chuckled. "And I still took a hell of a gamble. Few people are honest anymore. I had no idea if you were."

"But Gretchen, Tom, Liza," I choked out their names at the gruesome memories. "Why assault the teenage kitchen girl? Why kill the two owners? Why harm innocent people?"

Reaper pulled away from me like he touched a hot stove. His face twisted from lighthearted desire to something resembling shock and rage. And maybe even hurt.

I was even more stunned as he turned and left without another word, Hades' claws clicking on the ground after him.

MARIPOSA

Three days passed without Reaper saying a word to me. I continued to stay at his house but barely saw him or Hades, for that matter. The two of them were so in sync, I wondered if the dog was pissed at me, too.

Thanks to Tessa making me her unofficial midwife, I was kept busy and could at least pretend Reaper's cold shoulder didn't bother me. I, along with Noelle, helped her declutter and clean for the baby's arrival. Without an ultrasound machine, I couldn't monitor her condition as accurately as I'd liked but made do with a stethoscope and old-fashioned feeling for the baby's movements. She was 31 weeks along by my estimations and the baby seemed to be healthy.

Despite Reaper's silent treatment at the back of my mind, I found myself happier while tending to Tessa than I had felt in years. Her sweetness and positivity were infectious. We often wore matching grins as we both felt the thumps and kicks from the baby's activity. I wanted to work in labor and delivery while in school, and those moments with her felt like I made it. My calling was answered. Until I remembered I had been taken to this biker gang compound against my will.

When not with Tessa and Noelle, I familiarized myself with the medic's office. After making note what everything was and where it was stored, I rearranged cabinets and drawers to give me quick access to what I'd need most in an emergency. Seconds or even fractions of seconds could mean the difference of life or death for someone. A former EMT told me that right before I left Texahoma.

I was so focused on my reorganizing, I didn't notice someone stepping into the office until I heard, "Oh hey, Mari."

My head snapped up to the open office door, where Gunner's tall, lean body filled up the doorframe. The light from outside illuminated the disheveled flyaways of his hair, giving him a golden haloed appearance. Once again, I wondered how such a bloodthirsty man could look so angelic.

"Hey," I replied, my task already forgotten. "Need something in here?"

"Yeah." He smiled sheepishly and held up an index finger covered in grease and blood with a deep gash across two of his knuckles. "Got a boo-boo. Can you kiss it better?"

A smile tugged at my lips. His face and the playful way he said that made it hard not to. But I steeled my features quickly enough to shoot him a scathing look.

"What did you do?" I turned on the water in the sink, ignoring his question about kissing it.

"I was just fucking around with some knives in the armory. Made a bad catch." He shrugged as if it were no more than a papercut.

"Well, come over here and wash it before you bleed all over the floor." I pointed to the antibacterial soap next to the running tap. "Use plenty of that and wash for at least five minutes. You don't want to give infection a chance to set in."

"Yes, ma'am," he grinned, walking up next to me to thrust his hands under the running water. "It's sexy when you tell me what to do."

I ignored that statement, too, choosing instead to rummage through some drawers while my insides fluttered.

"Depending how deep it is, you might need stitches," I said with my back turned.

"Whatever you say, Doc," he answered cheerfully, and even began whistling a tune as he scrubbed his hands.

"That doesn't look too bad," I remarked when I unflustered myself and turned back to look. "You might not need that sewn up after all. I thought I saw some adhesive here that'll work..."

"You've got everything you need here, then?" he asked, for once not teasing me.

"Oh, yeah." I remembered he was the one who restocked all the supplies. "It's everything a medic could need, short of a major surgery. Thank you."

"No problem," he seemed genuinely pleased.

"Reaper always likes to think ahead. I don't know medical supplies that well, but I know some people who do. If there's anything else you need, just let me know." His grin turned lascivious. "And I do mean *anything*."

I heard his innuendo loud and clear, but the mention of Reaper's name turned my mood sour again. I missed him and that fucking annoyed me. I actually liked talking to him and the feeling seemed to be mutual. And after a dry spell of well over a year, I craved those skilled hands of his and the way his mouth claimed mine. It felt like my lips and my skin reawakened after a long dormancy and ached for real, human, non-medical contact.

I worked in tense silence as I cleaned Gunner's hand, the touch no longer clinical in my mind. With all his teasing and innuendo, my thoughts wandered to how *his* hands could make me feel. He had long, slender fingers on large palms. Small scars dotted across his knuckles, one stretching from the back of his palm to his wrist. Probably from many other mishaps with weapons, or incidents of violence that his angelic face would never give away.

"There's something between you and him, huh?" he mused, breaking the silence.

"Who?" I mumbled distractedly as I closed his wound with the surgical adhesive.

"You know who." I looked up to his playful blue eyes. "Reaper."

I huffed out a sigh as I released his hand and turned to the sink to wash my own. "Hard to have something between us when he pretends I don't exist."

My shoulders went up as I cringed hard at the words I couldn't take back. Could I sound any more like a stupid girl with a crush? I wasn't even supposed to *like* any of these guys.

"Oh shit," Gunner breathed. "So I guess you haven't heard the news, huh?"

"What news?" I shut off the water and looked up at him.

A smile overtook his mouth. "We're riding out tomorrow morning. And you're coming with us."

FIFTEEN

GUNNER

"What?" Her mouth fell open and it looked pretty damn cute, I had to admit. "Riding out where? And why am *I* coming?"

"We're scoping out an outpost at the base of the Sandia Mountains, since we're no longer doing business with the service center near Old Phoenix," I said. "It'll be a couple days' ride. And you're coming because you're the club medic. We're potentially going through enemy territory and would like to survive."

"Wait, hold on." Mari's brow furrowed as she waved her hands in front of us. Damn, was there anything she did that wasn't adorable as hell? "Since when am I the club medic?"

I lifted an eyebrow and spread my hands out to the sides, the injured one throbbing just slightly.

"You're still here, aren't you?"

Mari huffed out a sigh that puffed her cheeks out and levitated a strand of dark brown hair in front of her face.

"I guess. When was this decided?"

"At Church this morning," I told her. "Reaper said for you to pack the essentials, but keep it light. It's going to be a long ride, even for us."

"Who's going?" She almost looked as though she feared the answer.

"Us four," I counted off my fingers. "Me, Reap, Jandro, and Shadow. Hades and Horus, of course. You, plus four of my guardsmen."

"So eleven of us, including the animals." She tapped her chin thoughtfully as her eyes drifted over the cabinets. I smiled, crossing my arms as I watched her think about what to pack. She was already one of us, even if she didn't know it yet.

"The animals are full-fledged club members, too," I chuckled. "Definitely can't forget about them."

"Reaper's gonna be thrilled about being stuck with me for days," she grumbled. "Especially if Hades still likes me."

So I was right—they *did* have something between them. I had my suspicions at the barbecue, and doubly so after he stepped in at Fight Night. Reaper practically spat through his teeth that we'd need to bring her on this ride. He didn't specify what happened, but I knew him half my life and never saw him get this worked up over a woman before. Mari barely found her footing with us and they were already fighting like an old married couple.

"Hey," I lifted her chin with a finger, bringing those pretty hazel eyes to meet mine. "I don't like seeing you down about Reap. Know what'll make him crazy?"

"What?"

"Ride with me," I winked at her. "Or Jandro. Hell, even Shadow. But if you touch the big guy, he might spontaneously combust. Women don't really go near him, and I'm not sure he'd know what to do."

She laughed softly at that, and I swore my fucked up finger throbbed even faster.

"Riding with one of you guys is probably my only option. I don't think he wants me anywhere near him."

Damn Reaper. I just might have to kick his ass for that. I wasn't the type to always sympathize with women like one of those pussywhipped white knights, but I legitimately felt for Mari. She was just doing her job and never wanted to be here in the first place. Then she was thrown into Fight Night and bore the brunt of Reaper's cold shoulder all in the same hour. That shit would be rough, even to a man in the same circumstances.

"Don't worry about Reap," I told her, unable to resist dragging my finger from her chin down her neck. "He does this shit sometimes. Stick with me and Jandro and we'll keep you smiling."

There it was again, the smile she tried to hide. She really didn't want to let us think she was happy here, but we'd show her in time how much she really belonged with us.

"I just have one rule," I said, reluctantly letting my hand fall away from the contact with her skin.

Her eyebrows lifted. "What's that?"

"No trying to escape," I grinned and winked as I turned to leave the office.

———

THE POOL DECK was quiet that night. The air had cooled down significantly, making steam rise off the surface of the heated water. Steam mixed with the smoke puffed from fat cigars, the cherried ends looking like red eyes in the dim outdoor light.

"Nice of you to join us," Reaper remarked when I sat down, his cigar already halfway to ash.

"Had to finish packing the shit. Our gifts are fragile and I'm trying to sleep in tomorrow." I grabbed a cigar from his lacquered wooden box and stuck it between my teeth, then struck a match and began puffing.

"What did we decide on for a gift?" Jandro asked. His cigar looked barely started. The man liked to savor the finer things, which I always respected about him.

"An array of weapons that benefits mountain dwellers," I said with my first exhale. "A few of the nicer bows. Arrows with ceramic tips, that's the fragile part. Throwing knives, double-headed axes. Primitive stuff, but the Sandia outposters should appreciate it."

"Am I missing something?" Jandro asked critically, dark eyes narrowed and smoke exhaling from his nostrils like a bull.

"Like what?" I asked calmly. I respected Jandro as VP and for his ability to think outside the box, but that didn't give him the right to question my expertise.

"What's with the cowboys and Indians shit?" he asked. "Why not sniper rifles and silencers? A lot more effective, and you know, keeping up with the twenty-second century."

"Because the Sandian outpost people are isolated," I explained after a deep drag. "They're holed up in the fucking mountains. They need weapons that can be reused over and over again, and that don't need ammo because who knows when they'll get another supply? Even if this works out, we can't supply them *and* General Tash's rebellion with modern weapons. It'll wipe us out. I can't get it from my supplier any faster."

"I'm just concerned about this deal going sour because we insult them with weapons from fucking three hundred years ago," Jandro said. "I mean, Tash wants fucking stealth drones now. And we're giving guys two hundred miles away bows and arrows?"

"I know what I'm doing," I assured him. "The mountain dwellers are old-timers who appreciate the skill that goes into old-school weapons. They wouldn't know what to do with drones. If they're interested in guns, too, we'll work that out. But we also don't want to spoil them with a gift that's too nice right away."

Jandro looked at Reaper, whose cigar became little more than a nub during our conversation. "What say you, boss?"

"I trust Gunner's judgment," Reaper answered, setting his spent cigar in the ashtray and picking up his whiskey. "He's never done us wrong before. But we'll proceed with caution. For all we know, Razor Wire may have gotten to them already."

"I doubt that," I remarked. "Sadistic bastards don't know how to play nice with anyone."

Jandro nodded his agreement before he carefully

snuffed out his cigar and placed the remainder back inside Reaper's box.

"And with that, gentlemen, I'll say goodnight. Gotta make sure Shadow hasn't destroyed half the shit in my house again."

"The fuck?" I coughed up a cloud of smoke in surprise. "I thought he was drinking until he passed out every night?"

Jandro shook his head. "It's just making his tolerance go up higher and higher. Last night I woke up to him sleepwalking and his bedroom looked like a bomb hit. Just broken shit everywhere," he sighed, rising to his feet. "I feel bad for the guy. I know he can't help it but fuck. I'm getting tired of replacing broken shit, you know?"

"Maybe Mariposa has something he can take," I mused, thinking back to her cute smile and pretty blushing face. And the way she touched my hand while fixing up my cut. She didn't take me up on kissing it better, but I was satisfied with her blush and her smile.

"Mm, *Marrriposa*," Jandro said just before polishing off his glass of whiskey. "Why do I get the feeling she's either going to cure us of everything, or be the downfall of us four?"

"'Cause you've been watching too many old chick shows," Reaper scoffed.

"Hey, *Supernatural* is high quality entertainment, asshole! Doesn't matter if that shit is nealy a hundred years old now, it's fucking timeless."

"If you say so, dude," I chuckled as I exhaled smoke.

"Anyway," Jandro sighed. "See you boys in the morning."

Reaper and I mumbled our goodnights as he walked off toward his house, then a companionable silence fell over us. Reaper wasn't much of a talker. He was too busy thinking about, well, everything. But it was that kind of quiet, stoic leadership that earned him the title of president.

"Mariposa knows she's coming," I reported after a few moments. For some reason, I didn't feel right calling her Mari in front of him. It felt too familiar.

"You told her." Reaper stated it like an observation rather than a question.

"Yes," I answered. "Since you are apparently avoiding her."

He coughed out a dry laugh. "I knew someone would tell her. I just wasn't sure if it would be you or Jandro."

I chose not to answer, helping myself to a couple fingers of whiskey instead while feeling his eyes on me the whole time. No matter how cool I played it, he always saw through me.

"I don't mind, you know," he said in response to my silence.

"Mind what?" I allowed the whiskey to burn a trail of warmth to my stomach.

"Sharing her." His eyes smoldered. He was completely serious.

"What," I choked, "the fuck?"

"Only with you and Jandro." Reaper's lip curled. "As long as you remember she was mine first."

"Reaper, dude." I scrubbed a hand down my face, trying to make sense of this. He grew up with one mom and three dads, so I knew he was used to the whole sharing one woman thing, but that culty feminist shit was too fucking weird for me.

"I was just messing with her, man, " I told him. "Making her blush and smile and shit. I'm sure Jandro was, too. She's new and pretty, so it's just fun. I'm not trying to—"

"She should have more than one man," he continued, not looking at me anymore. It seemed more like he was talking to himself. "Mom would say she has the *hechiza*. I realized it the other day."

He lost me for good there. I shook my head. "Man, I know y'all got something more than just bumpin' uglies. I don't know how you can be willing to share her but not Heather."

Reaper returned his gaze to me with a scowl. "It's not the same as just passing a service girl around. A woman has to be worth bonding with multiple men. It's...sacred." He shifted in his chair. "Heather grew up in the same environment as me, but she doesn't hold those same qualities. Not to me, anyway."

I poured one more glass and downed it. Our fearless leader liked to wax philosophical sometimes, and I couldn't begin to comprehend everything going on in his head. I was a simple guy. I liked weapons, women, and getting a great deal. Reaper and Jandro could sometimes talk for hours about what led to the Collapse and life's other great mysteries but that shit was way over my head. So was the whole sacred woman mumbo jumbo.

"Thanks for the cigars, Reap." I ashed mine carefully and stood up. "I'll see you in the morning."

Aside from a small nod and a grunt, he barely seemed to notice I was leaving.

The street was quiet as I walked down the block to my house. Word must have spread that we'd be leaving early, so everyone likely turned in around midnight. Even Reaper's house up the street was dark. Neither Mari nor his sister seemed to be waiting up for him.

Horus was asleep on his perch when I walked in. I wasn't sure how he knew, but he always liked to sleep a lot before flying with us on long rides.

Peeling off my clothes and crashing into bed with a groan, I already knew sleep wouldn't come easy. Getting on my beast of a bike always amped me up like a shot of adrenaline. I couldn't wait to feel the roar of my baby vibrating with power again.

And if I played my cards right, I'd have a sexy woman holding onto me, too.

SIXTEEN

MARIPOSA

"You'll need chaps and a jacket." Noelle's bedroom looked like her closet vomited clothes everywhere. "And a helmet, not that the guys ever wear them. Mine should fit you."

"Jesus, Noelle," I huffed, sagging under the weight of all the riding gear she piled into my arms. "Aren't I going to melt under all this black leather?"

"Nah, you'd be surprised," she said, rifling through more items. "When you're going fast and the wind is whipping all around you, it won't feel hot even if you're covered. And you'll keep the sand and dirt off you. Ah, here!" She tossed me a round, black helmet with a mirrored visor. I barely moved in time to catch it.

"Thanks," I mumbled. "For letting me borrow all this stuff. I promise I won't use everything of yours forever. I'll get my own eventually."

"Oh yeah?" Her eyebrows lifted as she began shoving everything back in her closet. "Does that mean you plan on staying?"

I bit my lip, not knowing how to answer that. I just felt bad for constantly using her stuff and didn't give my own future here much thought. Reaper clearly didn't want me around. I was all but waiting for the day he kicked me out of his house. After what Gunner told me yesterday, though, maybe he was more likely to dump me off somewhere on this trip. Thankfully I packed enough water, first aid supplies and dried food to last me a few days in the desert.

Noelle playfully thumped me on the shoulder when I didn't answer her question.

"Don't think about it too hard," she teased. "But that is my best jacket, so make sure you bring it back."

"I will," I promised, knowing I'd pay a courier to return it to her if I did in fact get dumped off.

She wrapped me in a hug and I was surprised how nice and comforting I found it.

"Have a good ride," she said. "Keep those boys in line."

"Yeah, right," I muttered to her amusement.

After sliding on her borrowed chaps, buckling her boots, and shrugging on her jacket, I shouldered my new medic pack and grabbed the helmet as I walked outside to the rumbling of idling engines.

Gunner's men chatted and mingled, drinking coffee in the cul-de-sac next to their bikes. Shadow sat astride his beast of a bike a bit farther away from everyone else, arms crossed and looking forward as though waiting to take off.

Jandro knelt next to the bike I recognized as

Reaper's, tightening something with a wrench as I walked out.

"Damn, Mariposa," he grinned when he looked up, drinking me in slowly from head to toe. "You look like you were born to ride."

"Thanks." I wasn't sure if he was being genuine or making fun of me. Gunner's men turned to look at me, too, and right then I did feel hot as hell under all my gear.

"Ho-ly shit."

I turned to see Gunner himself walking up to me, and wanted to melt into the pavement. His hair was thrown up in a loose bun, dark goggles resting just above his forehead. His black cut looked like a tactical vest, lined with pockets for ammo and a holster on each side—each with a gun, of course. Horus sat perched on his shoulder, looking around with sharp eyes. Gunner's own eyes reminded me of the pool late at night, the clearest blue and shining.

"You look like you've been in the club your whole life," he grinned at me appreciatively.

"I was just telling her that," Jandro slapped a grease-covered hand to Gunner's chest. His smile said he was joking but I swore a spark of warning lit up his gaze.

"Good shit," Gunner responded coolly. "So, you riding with me, Mari? Or did this grease monkey beat me to that, too?"

"Um..."

Jandro's jaw ticked. He didn't otherwise look annoyed, but it only occurred to me then what they might be secretly competing for.

"Sure, I'll ride with you," I mumbled, my eyes bouncing back and forth between them, unsure what was customary. Could I offer to ride back with Jandro? Or was that weird?

"Perfect," Gunner beamed, draping a long arm over my shoulders as he directed me toward his bike. "Sorry, J. Can't win 'em all."

Jandro snorted as he returned to working on Reaper's bike. "If he gives you any shit, Mari, you come straight to me."

Gunner just chuckled. Even Horus made some soft screeches and chirps as if he was laughing.

"Put that helmet on and hop up." Gunner pulled his goggles over his eyes and threw one long leg over his seat. He throttled the engine as my much shorter legs climbed up behind him.

"Let me see that." He turned around and helped adjust my helmet, pulling the strap tight under my chin.

"Your finger looks better," I observed as he gently touched my face.

"Thanks to you," he smiled.

No sooner had he turned back around, Hades raced past us like a black blur. With a thunderous roar, Reaper's bike shot after him.

"Hold on tight, baby girl!" Gunner yelled over the growling motorcycles as they followed their president.

I wrapped my arms around his midsection just as we lurched forward and rode like the wind through the open gates.

I NEVER REALIZED how beautiful a dry, desert landscape could be until I saw it from the back of a motorcycle. It felt like we moved through an old postcard, complete with the mountains in the distance and saguaro cactus standing tall in the edges of the frame. When I flipped up the visor on my helmet, the landscape seemed to explode with color. The sky was a brilliant blue and clouds looked like cotton candy. Desert flowers gave off pops of pink and white. I could see now why these men loving riding so much.

In one of Gunner's mirrors, I spotted Shadow riding behind us. He wore no helmet or eye protection, and his hair flew out loosely behind him.

I squinted at the tiny reflection of the large man's face, curious about his features that he always covered with his hair. He seemed to have a large scar going through one eye. And I couldn't be sure, but it looked like his eyes were two different colors.

I inspected him in the mirror until one of Gunner's guards fell in line directly behind us, blocking my view.

We rode for most of the day, only stopping for the occasional piss breaks. I wandered out from relieving myself behind a bush at one point to see Reaper relaxing next to his bike.

His legs stretched out on the ground in front of him, head propped up against his rear tire, with Hades hanging off of his lap.

Reaper stroked down the length of the dog's back as affectionately as he would his own child. Hades rolled over to look up at his master with an open, tongue-lolling smile. Reaper smiled back and even appeared to murmur something to him. It was an oddly wholesome thing to see, this ruthless man treat an animal with so much gentleness.

Then he looked up at me and the smile dissipated into a scowl.

"Let's roll," he hollered, patting Hades' flank as he rose to his feet.

The men zipped themselves up, ended their rests, and hopped back onto their steeds to continue our journey. And the Steel Demons' president once again ignored my existence.

While the first several hours of the ride were scenic and fun, I was over it by the time dusk fell. My thighs and back ached again, although not nearly as badly as the first time.

Reaper led everyone a few miles off the main road, eventually stopping in a flat area with three saguaro cacti standing like guards over twenty feet high.

"We're about an hour's ride out from Razor Wire territory, so we should be safe camping here for the night," he said once all the engines cut. "I still want guards on rotating shifts. Gunner?"

"Got it, boss."

Horus, who had been perched on his handlebars, flew to the nearest cactus while Gunner's guardsmen spread out to begin patrols. In the meantime, Hades helped to dig out a fire pit while everyone else set up tents and bedrolls.

I unpacked Gunner's stuff while he checked out the area with his men and gave orders for patrols.

"Mariposa," Jandro called. "Come have dinner with me by the fire."

I hesitated. "You're not going to trick me into kissing you again, are you?"

Two of Gunner's men snorted with laughter before quickly moving out of the vice president's way. Jandro cast them a momentary glare before returning a warm gaze back to me.

"I'll be on my best behavior," he promised with a palm to his chest. "Unless something happens in which I need another good luck kiss."

"Stephan had no chance against you in that fight," I said, making my way toward him.

"I didn't expect him to challenge me." Jandro unwrapped a cloth bundle from his saddlebag and held out a piece of jerky to me. "He did good, though. I went easy on the kid. He'll be a good soldier."

I accepted the dried meat strip and took a bite, chewing thoughtfully as I watched the rest of the men set up camp. Shadow set himself up alone far away from everyone else, as usual. He pulled a handle of liquor from his saddlebag and sat down on his bedroll. The jerky nearly fell out of my mouth as I watched him chug straight from the bottle.

"Holy shit, is he trying to kill himself?"

"No," Jandro sighed. His fingers skimmed across my lower back. "Have a seat, Mari."

I lowered myself onto a flat rock, still watching in disbelief as Shadow made quick work of the alcohol.

"He'll be dead in five years if he keeps that up."

"And he'll probably welcome it," Jandro muttered,

setting up a cooking grate over the fire. "Shadow's been through shit none of us can even imagine."

He hesitated, glancing once more at his silent friend before continuing to set up. "He has nightmares where he wakes up screaming. The only way he and all of us can get a few hours of peaceful sleep is if he passes out from booze." His eyes lifted toward his silent friend. "And the big guy needs to put *a lot* of it away for that to happen."

"I have sleep aids," I said, reaching for my pack. "Side effects are minimal and he'll be—"

Jandro shook his head, looking at me with sorrow in his warm eyes. "No offense, Mari, but you're a woman. Shadow doesn't trust any women. The reasons why are complicated, but it's best you don't try to give him anything. At least for a little while."

His bottle now empty, the large man began swaying where he sat. He looked around the camp, but his one uncovered eye didn't seem to register what was around him. His lips began moving as if muttering to himself, which made Jandro spring into action.

"I'll be right back," he said, taking long strides to his friend.

No sooner had he knelt by Shadow's side, an arm fell over my shoulder and Gunner's smile beamed in front of my face.

"Aww, thanks for setting us up, baby girl! Keep doing that shit and I'll make you my old lady. Reaper will pitch a fit."

Said president and Hades were across the fire with Jandro and Shadow, talking softly among themselves while Shadow looked as though he struggled to stay awake.

But something the golden, smiling man said pulled my attention back to him.

"Set *us* up?" I blinked.

"Well, yeah. Where did you think you were gonna sleep? Not in the dirt by yourself."

"I, um..."

Gunner's smile faded as he slowly removed his arm from around my shoulders.

"Hey, you can relax. I remember how freaked out you were at the service center. I won't touch you like that again, not if it scares you." A lopsided grin returned. "I like weapons and dangerous shit, but I honestly don't want to scare anyone that doesn't deserve it. You've kinda been through a lot, so I get it."

I stared into the fire as I turned his words over in my head. "There's not a lot that scares me anymore, to be honest." Crackles and pops from the flames filled the silence. "But yeah, getting kidnapped and violated by a bunch of men on motorcycles is pretty high up there."

"We don't do that. Not the violating part, at least."

"You're the second man in this club who's told me that," I mused. "And with every day that passes, I want to believe you, but..." Gretchen's face haunted me every time I closed my eyes. How ashamedly she asked me for a morning-after pill.

Gunner scooted away from me with his eyes downcast, and I felt like I kicked a puppy.

"Well, you don't have to sleep near me if you don't want to. You can have my bedroll and I'll sleep on my leathers or something. I gotta be up for my patrol shift in a few hours, so—"

Goddamn it.

"Wait," I grabbed his arm, an apology stuck in my throat but it wouldn't come out. He almost *did* force himself on me back at the service center so why was I the one apologizing? One of these men *did* hurt Gretchen, but something at the back of my brain believed that it wasn't him.

"Maybe we can just sit next to each other first?" I suggested. "Just talk, and you know, get used to each other?"

That electrifying grin returned and my heart skipped a beat.

"You've been in my seat and holding onto me all day, baby girl. What's it gonna take for you to get used to me?"

"Tell me about you," I suggested. "I've been with you guys for almost a week and feel like I hardly know any of you. Where are you from? How'd you find Horus?"

"Now there's a story in both of those answers." He relaxed once again next to me. "I was Arizona born and bred, but my family's from California originally."

"Really? Before it sank into the ocean?"

"Yup, my grandparents were actors." He laced his hands behind his head. "They lived in Hollywood and did a few movies before that whole area went under. My parents were little when they headed east to evacuate."

"I heard you can swim out there and still see whole towns and neighborhoods underwater."

"I wouldn't," Gunner chuckled. "My folks said the

pollution is so toxic, you'll get cancer just by letting the water touch you. I heard the coastline is pretty, though." He paused as he looked at me. "Maybe we can ride out there one day."

"Maybe," I mused.

"As for Horus," he continued. "I was bird-hunting, quite ironically. Not for falcons, though. For quail. Out of nowhere, this fluffy little fucker with big-ass talons starts clinging to my pantleg and screaming bloody murder. I knew he was some kind of raptor based on his feet, so I fed him some quail I shot. He's pretty much never left my side ever since." He nodded across the fire to Reaper. "Him and Hades have a similar story. Hades was an abandoned pup and they just seemed to find each other."

The dog rested calmly on the ground, his dark eyes blinking slowly with sleepiness while his owner continued talking with Jandro and Shadow.

"Does Horus do anything...unusual, like Hades?"

"Like what?"

"You know, like how Hades can just run alongside Reaper's bike for hours. No normal dog can do that."

"Hmm," Gunner pursed his lips as he thought. "I guess I never really thought about it. No, Horus seems like a pretty normal bird to me. Sometimes I have dreams like I'm flying, though, and it's like I'm seeing through his eyes. Hey," he tapped my arm with the back of his palm, looking excitedly at me like a little kid. "What's the freakiest dream you've ever had?"

"Oh, that's easy," I laughed. "In nursing school, I dreamed I delivered a two-headed baby."

"No shit! How did you react?"

"I just started talking to it and the baby talked back! But each head answered in a different language. I think one of them was Russian."

Gunner howled with laughter. We talked until the fire burned down to embers, and I didn't think twice about following him to his tent and falling asleep next to him on his bedroll.

SEVENTEEN

MARIPOSA

I distinctly remembered how the temperature dropped during the night. So I was surprised to find myself in a cocoon of warmth when dawn approached.

Or rather, a sandwich of warmth.

My eyes fluttered open, expecting to see Gunner's fair, angelic features. Instead I found caramel skin and Jandro's full lips inches away from me.

With a gasp, I tried to push away but my back pressed against something solid. Looking over my shoulder, there was the angelic face I expected to see. And damn, did he look sweet in his sleep.

Gunner's lips were parted as he breathed softly, his hand resting on my thigh while Jandro's arm draped over my waist.

Turning back to the VP, his jaw was tight and his brow furrowed in his sleep. His fingers also periodically clenched around my shirt. Seeing how differently these two men slept was morbidly fascinating to me.

"Jandro?" I whispered, placing a tentative hand on his bicep.

"Huh!"

He jerked awake at my touch, sitting straight up immediately.

"Uh, hi," I said meekly.

He looked at me and only then did his expression relax. "Morning, Mariposa," he sighed while rubbing his temples.

"You all right?"

"Yeah, yeah." He shot me a sheepish grin. "I'm not an easy sleeper, that's all. Didn't mean to scare you."

"Can I ask what you're doing in Gunner's tent?"

The hand resting on my thigh wrapped around my waist in reply.

"I asked him to come," Gunner murmured sleepily at my back. "I didn't want to leave you alone during my patrol shift. But when I came back, the fucker wouldn't leave."

"You had your head on my chest. It was the sweetest thing," Jandro teased. "No way was I gonna move and disturb you."

"Wow." I drew my knees up to my chest. The cozy warmth of their bodies turning into a stifling heat all over me. "I must have been really out of it."

"Riding is exhausting if you're not used to it." Jandro's eyes brightened. "And you get to do it all over again today."

"Great," I grumbled, stretching my arms and legs out. I felt a little soreness in my limbs but nothing too bad.

"Aw, you'll be fine." Gunner sat up and kissed the back of my head before I could react. "We'll get some coffee and breakfast in you, then you'll be right as rain, baby girl."

He rose to his feet and exited the tent, leaving me to stare wide-eyed at Jandro.

"All you're missing's a kiss from Shadow now, huh?" He laughed as my eyes surely doubled in size. "Relax, you don't have to worry. He's not really the kissy type."

"So, uh..." Eager to focus on something else, I pulled a rubber band off my wrist and started tying my hair up. "How is he this morning?"

"Fine," Jandro shrugged. "Probably up early and packed before all of us. He doesn't get hangovers and never sleeps more than he has to."

"Really?"

"Yeah. I'm jealous, to be honest," he chuckled before going quiet. "You riding with golden boy again today?"

"I'm not sure," I admitted. "He hasn't asked me yet."

Jandro's eyes brightened. "Want to ride with me?"

"Um, sure."

"It's a comfortable ride, I promise," he winked. "My baby's made for long distance. And I know her down to every gear. No rattles, no bumps. Just smooth sailing."

"Sounds good." A smile came to my mouth and he returned it.

"Great. I'll see you at breakfast." He made a sudden movement toward me, then stopped, hesitated, then turned and left the tent.

I was alone. Just me and my racing heartbeat. I

thought for a moment he was leaning in to hug or kiss me.

What would you have done?

Five days ago, I would have fought tooth and nail to get away from him. Now I slept between two of these men with no fear, and I wasn't so sure if I'd refuse him.

———

I PACKED up Gunner's tent and bedroll, putting everything away in his saddlebags when he brought me a tin mug of coffee and a bowl full of scrambled eggs, baked beans, and bacon bits.

"Jandro told me you're riding with him today, sly bastard. I gotta be faster next time."

"Just as long as you don't interrupt my beauty sleep to ask me to ride with you first," I joked.

"Wouldn't dream of it, baby girl," he said softly. Those bright blue eyes looked into mine long enough to make my stomach flutter. "Damn, Reaper has no idea what he's missing."

"What?" I blinked.

"Nothin'. Have a good ride." He reached out and stroked his thumb along my chin. "Wave at me if you want to switch off." Almost exactly like Jandro earlier, he paused as if considering something before walking away.

My stomach was doing almost too many flips to keep my breakfast down. What the hell was going on? Not just with them, but with me?

After finishing my food and washing out my dishes

with sand, I spotted Hades as I approached Jandro's bike, which was conveniently parked next to Reaper's.

The dog waited patiently next to his master's front wheel, looking at me with a cute head tilt as I pulled on my riding gear.

"Hey, good boy," I whispered.

His ears pricked forward as his rear end lifted off the ground. Wagging his stub of a tail, Hades only made it a few steps toward me when a high-pitched whistle stopped him in his tracks.

We both looked to see Reaper and Jandro walking side by side in our direction. Like usual, the former wore his signature scowl, the latter his flirtatious smile. Reaper walked right past me without even a glance, even ignoring Hades' puppy eyes for affection as he mounted his steed.

"Ready, Mari?" Jandro's fingertips lightly grazed my back as he moved in front of me.

"Yeah," I smiled back but he seemed to sense my uneasiness.

"Don't worry about him," he nodded up ahead to his president. "It's not you. He's stressed about this deal working out. Nothing should go wrong, but we need to tread carefully."

"What should I do?" I placed my hands tentatively on his waist as he sat in front of me. Although just as solid, his body was broader than Gunner's so I couldn't reach around as far.

He answered me by lacing his fingers through one of my hands and throwing me a look over his shoulder.

"Just be you."

————

THE MOUNTAINS in the distance grew larger and larger until the highest peak blocked out the sun. At the head of the pack, Reaper gradually slowed as the road became narrow and winding.

"Are those..." I squinted at the sight up ahead, nearly resting my chin on Jandro's shoulder as I tried to get a closer look. "...palm trees?"

"Haven't seen those in a while, have you?" he chuckled.

"I don't think I've ever seen a real one before."

"It's tacky as hell to see 'em now in the fuckin' desert," he yelled over his engine. "But they used to be signs of an oasis, a place for rest and relaxation. Resorts planted them so you could see them from miles away."

"Is this place a resort?"

"Used to be."

The road took us between the two skinny tree trunks standing out like sore thumbs. We soon came to a building at least six stories high and dotted with many balconies and large windows. It made the Old Phoenix service center look like a rundown shack.

Reaper slowed to a halt and everyone else stopped behind him. Leaving his bike running, he dismounted and nodded to Jandro, who looked over his shoulder and nodded at Gunner.

"The three of us are going in first," he slid off his bike with a gentle pat to my leg. "Shadow's got our backs. Watch him if anything happens."

"Why, what's gonna happen?"

He smirked at me. "Hopefully we'll get some comfy rooms and a dip in the pool. But we've got to play our cards right. It won't be more than a few minutes."

He paused to look at me once more, eyes casting down to my lips before walking off to meet Reaper. Gunner followed him, carrying a large metal case. He winked one blue eye at me as he passed, and the three men went through the front door.

I looked behind me at Shadow, the furthest one in the back. He was still astride his bike but with his feet on the ground and a large assault rifle in his hands. Looming tall over everyone and dressed entirely in black, he really did take after a shadow.

Minutes crawled by. No one spoke. Some of Gunner's guardsmen drifted their hands to the weapons at their hips or backs.

A flash of movement caught my eye. Flipping up the visor on my helmet, I craned my neck to look up at the balconies on the tallest floor. I thought I saw a curtain move but upon looking more closely, it was armed men walking back and forth on the roof. Gunner's men noticed them, too, only they didn't look up as obviously as I did.

After what felt like hours, Reaper, Jandro, and Gunner, now empty-handed, emerged from the building. The whole club seemed to let out a sigh of relief.

"Weapons down. We're cleared to stay," Reaper announced. "No women here, though. Y'all are either fucking each other or your hands tonight."

A few of the men groaned in disappointment. Big G looked especially perturbed.

Ignoring them, Reaper gave Hades a quick pat before getting back on his bike. "They're setting up for us inside now. We'll park in the garage."

"How'd it go?" I asked Jandro as he resumed his seat.

"Worried about me?" he teased with a smile. "It went well. The owner was cautious, naturally, but pleased with our offering. The real test is how hospitable they'll be during our stay."

"How long are we staying?"

"Two days, maybe three. Reaper wants to ensure they won't backstab us if we continue working together in the future."

We pulled into the garage, which looked like a converted horse stable, then entered the lobby through a side door.

"Wow," I breathed.

It was much nicer than my old service station, and definitely kept cleaner. They went all out on the desert palace theme with sandstone columns, an open floor plan with high ceilings, and tiled floors in an elegant pattern of earth tones.

The furniture consisted of low couches and floor cushions, with coffee tables lined with exotic-looking fruit. Gunner's men didn't hesitate in sprawling out over the comfortable seating and helping themselves to food.

Two young women rushed out from behind a curtain carrying pitchers of water and ale. My pulse sped up as the men's eyes crawled over them perversely. *Fucking hell, not here, too.*

"Have a seat, Mari," Gunner patted the cushion next

to him. Horus hopped off his shoulder and pecked curiously at some of the food on the table.

"It feels weird to be on this side of the table," I mused, easing into the seat next to him.

"Feels good, doesn't it?" He popped a grape into his mouth. "Riding all day long, then getting treated like royalty."

"Gun, get your bird off the table before it shits on the food."

We looked up together at who snarled the order. Reaper, of course. Acting like a crabby father after a long road trip.

Gunner let out a short whistle, and Horus immediately took off flying out the open door. "It's about time for him to hunt anyhow."

"Did you train him to do that?" I asked, helping myself to a few olives.

"No, more like he trained me on what sounds he would respond to."

We ate and relaxed for a few hours without incident. The bikers did little more than flirt and stare at the two kitchen girls, much to my relief. Once everyone was full of food and drink, Jandro left Reaper's side to sandwich me between him and Gunner again.

"They allotted us nine rooms based on our gifts for them," he glanced at Gunner. "That means you get your own room, Mari. If you want."

"Yes," I said, maybe a bit eagerly. I hardly had a moment to myself in days.

The guys exchanged a grin at that. "We'll still keep you between us, to be safe," Jandro said.

"And if you get lonely, just knock on a wall." Gunner squeezed my waist, his lips nuzzling near my ear. "Preferably mine."

My resulting squirm from the contact pressed me right up against Jandro's shoulder. A giggle bubbled out of my chest before I could suppress it.

"You can knock on his wall if you like, but," the VP's fingertips grazed my lower back, "you know where to go for a nice spooning."

"Spooning?" I laughed, turning to look at him. "Is that what they're calling it now?"

Jandro shrugged, his expression innocent but the heat in his eyes anything but. "Cuddling. Canoodling. Cupcaking. Whatever you want to call it. I just want more of that sweetness from last night."

"Is that *all*?" I lifted my eyebrows. "I'm surprised."

"I'm full of surprises," he returned.

The two of them touched me with abandon now, and the flirty banter only escalated with each passing day. As time went on, my resistance to it only grew weaker. My insides felt like hundreds of fluttering butterfly wings.

This felt like a luxury I couldn't afford. These men were to be feared, not flirted with. They could hold me down and take what they wanted at any moment. So why bother with all this, the teasing and flirting? I wondered as everyone started getting up, dispersing down the walkways to their rooms. Jandro and Gunner led me between them, of course.

"Reaper gets the nicest suite, naturally," Jandro said. "Which means Gun and I get the second nicest." He looked at me and grinned. "Last chance to pick a room with your favorite."

"I'll be fine in my own room, really." I squeezed the straps of my pack on my shoulders, eager for some privacy. These guys were affecting my ability to think too much.

"Suit yourself," Gunner shrugged, opening a door. "Knock on your right wall," he added with a wink before going in.

"I'll be at the pool if you'd like to join me," Jandro offered from his door on the other side of me.

"Maybe later. I think I'm going down for a nap," I yawned.

Try as I might, I couldn't shut my brain off, no matter how exhausted my body was. The room was comfortable and spacious, but I couldn't bring myself to relax.

Frustrated, I decided to get up and take a walk. I didn't even make it to the end of the hallway when my heart jumped into my throat.

Through the doors at the end of the corridor, leaning over the balcony in a cloud of cigar smoke, stood Reaper.

I almost turned around and headed back to my room. His cold-shouldering since Fight Night hurt more than any of those punches I took. Why subject myself to that again?

Then again, why bring me all this way if he was just going to treat me like mud on his boot? I was fucking tired of waiting around for him to talk to me again. And as I forced my steps to proceed onward through those doors, it scared me how much I missed him.

Hades' ears perked up when I opened the door, but he remained sitting at his master's feet. Sometimes the two of them acted like independent beings, but right then they seemed to share the same mind.

Reaper's shoulders didn't even stiffen as I walked up next to him, leaning my forearms on the railing in the same posture.

"How long is this going to go on for?"

He took a long drag on the cigar and exhaled as if I hadn't said a word.

"I don't know what you mean," came his gruff, eventual reply.

"Are you kidding me?" I couldn't bring myself to be patient. I'd been patient for five fucking days already. "This. The silent treatment. Making me part of your club but acting like I don't exist. You can't keep this up forever."

"Watch me."

"Reaper, I-I don't get it." My voice cracked and I could barely bring myself to say the next part. "One minute you're...kissing me." It felt like so long ago, I began to question if it really happened. "The next, you're acting like I'm this huge inconvenience in your life. If you don't want me around, that's fine." It wasn't fine, not anymore. But he didn't need to know that. "One of the guys can drop me off in any podunk town between here and Sheol."

"That's not gonna happen." His teeth clenched on

the cigar. "As much as I'd like to dump your ass in the middle of the desert, I need a medic."

Ow, fuck.

"Okay," I said cautiously. "So why—"

"Why do you fucking care?" he growled, turning to face me for the first time in days. " You see me as a murderer and a rapist. Aren't I doing you a favor by leaving you the hell alone?"

His words flung out at me from some deep, painful place. Too stunned to reply, I could only back away a few steps.

"Yeah, that's what I thought," he grumbled.

"I don't know, I—" My mind raced as I tried to reconcile the horrors he committed with the man who treated his animal companion so gently. "As I'm spending more time in the club, I'm starting to think, I dunno. Maybe you guys aren't all bad."

"Not all bad?" he laughed cruelly as he flicked the butt of his cigar, sending ashes raining down over the balcony. "Sugar, you haven't *seen* how bad we can be. We're the stuff nightmares are made of." He leaned in close to me. "The Collapse took all your rights away, but for men like me? We thrive in this world. A lawless land means *I* make the laws. And I'll dispense justice in any way I see fit."

His words swung heavily through the air as if made of battle axes, and my heart dropped in much the same way.

"So I was right about you," I said, nearly choking on my sadness. "My first impression, anyway." Nevermind if *he* never forced himself on anyone, or that his hands felt like magic or his kiss took my breath away. Reaper was the living embodiment of the Collapse itself. Cruelty, violence, and chaos wrapped in a sinfully beautiful package.

"Yeah," he scoffed, turning his bitter gaze back to the mountain view. "You were right about me."

With nothing else to say, I turned to leave. Hades' dark eyes followed me, wide and puppy-like as I reached for the door. I would've loved the company of a friendly, nonjudgmental animal since the surrounding humans proved to be just as awful as I thought. But I knew better than to touch Reaper's dog.

"None of us touched her, you know."

I froze a moment before slipping through the doorway, then whipped around to stare at his broad back.

"What?"

"The kitchen girl," he said, tossing the finished end of his cigar over the balcony. "Tom was the one who abused her while his cunt of a wife watched it happen without lifting a finger to help. He made no secret about wanting to do the same to you."

EIGHTEEN

REAPER

I shouldn't have told her. I should have let her keep on believing I was just another barbaric piece of shit senselessly killing whoever got in my way. At least then she'd feel better about not talking to me.

She was all I thought about as I rode out with Jandro the next morning, which really pissed me off because I needed to keep my head in the game. No woman ever succeeded in distracting me from my duties as much as her.

We were in foreign territory and I couldn't shake the feeling that something was fishy about this deal. It all went according to plan, but Hades' hackles had been permanently raised since we got here. His whole body was tense and he'd been growling more than usual. I swore he hadn't slept at all last night. Every time I woke up he was staring at the door, alert and on-guard.

"No sign of Razor Wire or any other club," Jandro said as we stopped at a ridge overlooking a canyon below. "Gun said Horus hasn't seen anything either. I dunno what to tell you, Reap."

"They're fucking us, somehow," I insisted, raising a canteen of water to my lips. "They wouldn't have gone along with the deal so easily if they weren't."

"Maybe our reputation does precede us," my VP smirked. "Word travels faster now that borders don't mean much. It's not just the Arizona-Utah territory that knows who we are."

"Nah," I shook my head. "There's always a bigger fish and Razor Wire used to be it."

"Til General Tash captured 'em," Jandro reminded me. "And Tash has always been honest with us."

"Yeah, but Razor's a slippery bastard. This area used to be loyal to him. I wouldn't be surprised if he had multiple failsafes in the event of his capture."

"Come on, Reap." Jandro leaned against his steed as he crossed his arms. "What's really got your asscheeks clenched? Mariposa?"

"You son of a horse fucker."

"Hey, don't get mad at me. You're the one being a moody bitch while she's doing the best she can in this situation."

I wanted to throw something over the edge of the cliff. I needed my water canteen for the ride back so I settled on a fist-sized rock on the ground and hurled it over the ridge.

"Feel better?" Jandro asked.

Who died and made you my fucking therapist?

"I told her the truth," I admitted. "About why we killed Tom and Liza."

"And?" he inquired. "Did y'all kiss and make up?"

"No."

The only sound that followed was the wind blowing through the canyon.

"But that's what you were hoping would happen," Jandro piped up after a few moments.

"Nah." I sealed up my water and returned it to my saddlebag. "I stopped hoping anything good would come my way years ago."

"Okay, so you didn't want her believing the rumors about you, which is almost the same thing," he concluded. "You want her to know the *real* you."

"You overestimate me, Jandro." I threw a leg over my seat and maneuvered my baby back to the road. "All I want is to ride and see another day long enough to smoke a cigar. Pussy's fine, too, but I don't give two shits what a woman thinks of me."

Jandro laughed, shaking his head at the sky as he followed me. "Oh, I know you much better than that, Reap."

———

THE SIGHT of Mariposa lying on a deck chair next to the pool didn't help to prove my point at all.

"Fuck." I sucked my bottom lip between my teeth and felt all the blood rush to my dick.

She wore one of my sister's bikinis, which honestly fit Mari much better. I didn't know how the fuck women's clothing worked except that the red polka-dotted number accentuated, supported, and highlighted every delectable curve on her body. It was like magic. Or maybe it was just her body that was magical, or the fact that I hadn't fucked anyone in nearly three weeks.

Her lips curved into a smile as she watched Gunner do a flip off the diving board. Lips that I kissed, that tasted sweeter than the wild blackberries I picked as a child.

Jandro punched me in the shoulder, and the resulting grin he shot at me made me want to punch him in the face.

"Getting in?" He was already shrugging off his cut and pulling his T-shirt up. "I bet Hades will love it."

"Nah, later," I said. "I can't think straight around all you fucks."

"Or you're just thinking with the wrong head." His eyes slid appreciatively over Mariposa. "Not that I blame you."

I headed into the main building before he could give me any more shit, Hades loyally trotting at my side. Before I could talk myself out of it, I went up to the smoker's lounge and fished another cigar out of my cut pocket.

I didn't normally have more than one at the end of a long day, but this place seemed to wreak havoc on my nerves. Nothing looked suspicious, so why did I feel the need to look over my shoulder constantly?

Hades guarded the door like usual as I lit up. Daren would have pitched a fit if he knew I was smoking two cigars a day. His sire passed away in his early fifties from esophageal cancer. I was fourteen and Daren was twelve. As the youngest of us, he'd been sheltered from the pile of shit the world was becoming. His sire was the first of my fathers to go, and our lives only descended deeper into the shit pile since then.

"Would you really be so upset if we saw each other again soon?" I said to the empty room. "You're gone because I fucked up. A year later and I'm still willing to trade, if anyone's listening. It should've been me, Daren."

How ironic that I earned the name Reaper and couldn't even bargain for my little brother's death.

Hades' wet nose nudging my hand lifted me out of my guilt, if just for a moment.

"How do you always know, boy?" I scratched his ears as I looked into those deep, soulful eyes. "Whenever I think about him or talk like he's here, you just know."

"Excuse me, sir?"

I looked up, annoyed at the intrusion. In my rush to light up and be alone, I left the door to the lounge open. One of the kitchen girls poked her head through.

"Yes?" I snapped.

"Mr. Fischlin would like a word with you in his office. At your earliest convenience, sir."

"Regarding what?" I demanded. "The gift from yesterday?"

"I'm not privy to that knowledge, sir. But he requested that you come alone." Her eyes fell to Hades, who gave her a low, rumbling growl. "You may bring your animal companion if it suits you."

"It does suit me," I carefully ashed my cigar. "He goes everywhere with me. Tell Mr. Fischlin I'll be up shortly."

She left to deliver my message while I observed Hades' behavior. He was in full-fledged guard dog mode, which set my own alarm bells ringing. And wanting me alone? How obvious could Fischlin be?

I left the lounge and considered swinging by the pool to signal the guys something was up, but Fischlin's marksmen in the corridors made me think twice.

They looked casually posted enough but I felt their eyes raking over me like a woman's hands. A stolen glance told me a few of the higher-ranking ones already equipped the ceramic arrowheads we gave them yesterday. These fuckers didn't waste any time. If I tried to alert my men, they'd return our gifts right through our hearts. I wasn't about to take good men down with me, so I headed straight for Fischlin's office.

I kept my pace casual, my face neutral, while I tried to form a plan. Even Hades was able to relax his body language walking at my side. If only I knew what that brain of his sensed in the air.

It didn't help that Fischlin's office was at the far end of the building, away from all the rooms and public areas. Alerting anyone without some big commotion would be nigh on impossible.

My gaze turned skyward, looking through the columns lining the outdoor walkway for Horus. Gunner and his bird seemed to have a similar bond as Hades and me, although I wasn't entirely sure what that entailed. If the raptor was out there and saw me, I could only hope Gunner would know, or feel, something.

With no sight of the bird, I looked ahead to

Fischlin's office door. My heart rate picked up and I fought the urge to quicken my pace. *Steady, steady.*

I never made it to his office.

Hades stopped in his tracks, bared his teeth and started barking wildly. His raised hackles gave him a humpbacked look.

"Easy, boy," I murmured to him, watching the marksmen nock their arrows in my peripheral vision. "Calm down. What is it?"

He kept fucking going. I never heard him bark so loudly before. It echoed off the columns and I had no doubt the others at the pool heard him.

"Hades!" I said with more force in my tone. "Quiet!"

He lunged at me in response, jaws open wide.

"What the—"

I was fucking stunned watching him come at me as if in slow motion. What the hell happened to my dog? He never attacked me. Even knowing full well how powerful those jaws were, I could never bring myself to hurt him. Not even to protect myself.

So I let him lunge at me. His teeth closed around my shirt and he twisted, pulling me to the ground with the strength of a two-hundred-pound man.

Not half a second later, the force of an explosion sent me rolling blindly across the desert ground. Heat singed the hairs on my skin as glass and rubble rained down on me.

NINETEEN

MARIPOSA

"Gunner, no!" I shrieked, flailing my arms and legs wildly. "Don't you dare!"

"Come on," he laughed devilishly. "The water feels amazing."

"I'll get in, just give me a second."

"No." His eyes flashed with the thrill of a predator on the hunt. "Now."

He lunged and I tried to dodge, but he was too fast for me. I only ran a few steps on the pool deck when his arm caught me around the waist. We spun around from the momentum until he leaned us over the edge, and we crashed into the crystal-blue water.

I remembered to hold my breath at the last possible second before the cold shock hit me. With how hot and dry it was, the water probably did feel good. I wouldn't know, not with the panic surging through my chest.

Rather than fighting Gunner in the cool, quiet underwater world, I clung to him like a raft. It must have been seconds, but felt like an hour before he kicked up to return us to the surface.

"See?" He flipped his hair back and grinned that pearly, boyish smile at me. "Feels great, doesn't it?"

"Yeah, about that." My legs wrapped like a vice around his waist, my arms clinging to his shoulders. "I can't swim."

"What?" His hands supported my lower back, a ghostly soft touch under the water. "How can you not swim?"

"I grew up in Middle of Nowhere, Texas, okay? Not a lot of swimmable bodies of water around."

He stared at me like I grew a third eye in the middle of my forehead.

"I don't think I've ever met anyone who couldn't swim. It's like second nature to me."

"Well, lucky you." I directed a small splash at him. "I hope giving CPR is second-nature to you, too, because I was about to need it."

"Sorry, Mari." His face fell. "I didn't know. I just figured everyone could."

"It's okay." I couldn't be mad at him for not knowing. Not with that adorable sad face he was giving me. "Just listen when a girl tells you *no* next time."

"Tell you what." His eyes brightened as he walked us to the shallow end. "I'll teach you how to swim if you teach me CPR." The devilish grin returned. "Especially if I get to practice mouth-to-mouth on you."

"Hmm, I'll have to think about it." I shot him a coy smile as I pulled myself out. "Show me how good of a swimmer you are while I dry off. I need to know if my teacher's qualified."

"Oh, you couldn't have picked anyone better." He began an elegant backstroke across the pool, eyes still locked on mine.

I settled into a deck lounger as he showed off, even doing flips off the diving board. My hair and skin were dry within minutes under the baking sun. The heat almost made me want to go back in the water just to cool off and cling to Gunner again.

Almost.

How long had it been since I just laid out in the sun, though?

Pushing away everything I learned in school about sun damage, I closed my eyes and basked in the heat. If I used my imagination a little, I could pretend I was on a beach vacation without a care in the world.

Murmuring voices pulled me out of the fantasy in my head, and I cracked my eyes open in curiosity.

Jandro and Reaper spoke in low voices as they walked between the columns of the elegant outdoor corridor, their heads bent toward each other as if discussing something important. Both had on their cuts as if they just returned from a ride.

My heart jumped at the sight of Reaper. Part of me wanted to hide, even underwater, while the other part wanted to march up to him and apologize.

What he told me on the balcony hit me like a base-ball bat to the stomach. I thought wrongly about him based on, well, nothing. And while he did awful things for his own and his club's survival, he wasn't the monster I thought he was.

I laid awake thinking about it all night last night rather than sleeping. And the one thought that stuck to the forefront of my mind was what Tessa said that night at the barbecue.

What if he didn't actually kidnap me, but rescued *me?*

My throat turned drier than the desert surrounding me. I gripped the armrests of my lounge chair, trying to get up the nerve to talk to him.

"Mari, watch me!" Gunner called gleefully like a child.

I put on a grin as he moonwalked across the diving board then backflipped into the water. When I looked over to the two club leaders again, Jandro removed his cut and was in the process of taking his shirt off while Reaper turned and walked in the opposite direction.

My heart sank as I watched his form grow smaller until he disappeared from view. Of course he didn't want to be around me, not after what I'd falsely accused him of. But it still stung.

"IIey, Mari." Jandro approached me with his signature flirtatious grin, cut and shirt thrown over his bare shoulder. "Careful laying out for too long or you'll get burned."

"I'm working my way up to your shade of tan." I watched him sink into the deck chair next to me, not a single tan line on his caramel torso. For a moment I wondered if his skin tasted as sweet as he looked.

"You can thank my Guatemalan parents for this tan," he chuckled, leaning back and stretching his legs out in front of him. "Arizona and Texas were the Far North to them, and y'all still sunburn like lobsters up here," he teased.

"My dad was from Mexico," I told him. "So I can get as dark as you, I just might have to work harder at it."

"Mm-hm," he smiled before looking out at Gunner's antics in the pool. "Your old man still around?" he asked gently.

"No," I answered, bringing my gaze up to the palm trees overhead. "He was fighting in the Texas border wars and never came home one day. Then my mom went to look for him, and she never came back either."

"Sorry," Jandro murmured. "I barely even remember my folks. I was raised by my aunt and uncle in Old Tucson."

My chest tightened. What the Collapse did to families was so overwhelmingly sad, I preferred to talk about anything else.

"Where did Reaper go?"

"Went to be alone," Jandro humored my subject change. "He gets in moods like that sometimes."

"I guess he's never really alone with Hades."

"Yeah," Jandro breathed. "Sometimes that dog is the only company he ever wants or seems to need."

BOOM!

An invisible force sounded like thunder crashing next to my ears and nearly knocked me off my chair. The ground shook so hard, pool water splashed up onto the deck.

"What the hell?" Jandro jumped up and stood over

me protectively, eyes narrowed and suspicious. "Gun, did you—"

"Oh my god!" I sprang to my feet at the sight of Gunner in the shallow end of the pool.

His head rested on the ledge, but his eyes had completely rolled back until only the whites were visible. He twitched slightly, his mouth going from open and slack to tightly clenched. And every small jerk of his head sent him closer to slipping underwater.

"Gunner!" I went to run to him but Jandro braced his forearm across my stomach and pulled me back. "He's having a seizure!" I yelled. "He could drown, let me go!"

"He's okay, Mari," he answered with unusual calm. "It's just something that happens, you'll see. Something else is going on, though. Fucking Reaper was right."

I didn't have a moment to think about what he said when a commotion on the roof brought our attention skyward.

One of the guards, armed with a bow and arrow, was desperately trying to fight off a bird. The animal hovered around him, too close for him to shoot with the bow, and darted down with its talons outstretched toward the man's face. His arms and hands were already bloodied and torn up as he raised them to shield his face.

"Is that...Horus?" I shielded my eyes as I watched.

"Get Mari out of here!"

Gunner, now looking perfectly fine, swam like a dolphin across the pool and hopped out right in front of us, his expression hard and jaw clenched. "We've been fucking set up. They're coming this way right now. We can't let them capture a woman, let alone our only medic."

"How many did you see?" Jandro demanded.

"At least twenty."

"Any sign of Reaper?"

"No."

"What the—!"

Jandro hoisted me over his shoulder without another word, carrying me to the sandstone brick wall that surrounded the pool area.

"Climb over, Mari," he instructed.

"No! What's going on?"

He lifted me up by the waist so I had no choice but to grab the top of the wall and hoist myself up.

"There's no time to explain," Gunner told me apologetically. "But you've got to hide and they can't find you under any circumstances, do you understand?"

"Stay out of sight of the men with bows and arrows," Jandro added, his hand lingering on my leg that dangled over. "Do *not* try to sneak back in, no matter what they do to us."

"What do you mean?" I demanded. Fucking hell, what was happening?

"When we break out, we'll come for you." Gunner, the taller of the two of them, reached up to stroke his thumb along my jaw. "We'll explain everything later. But in the meantime, you can't let them find you. No matter what. Promise us, Mari."

If I wasn't in danger of falling off this thin ledge, I

would've leaned down to kiss him. Or hell, both of them.

"I promise." The words came out a shaky whisper.

"Good girl." Jandro flashed me a tight smile. "Now go."

I didn't know whose lives I feared for more, theirs or my own. At some point, I found myself caring for these men. I just didn't realize it until right then.

With a final look at their tense faces, I swung my bare leg over the wall and carefully lowered myself down the other side until they disappeared from view.

Now outside the grounds of the outpost, wild brush, sparse trees, cactus, and a rocky ravine greeted me. The best part? I was still in a bikini with worn out sandals as footwear.

"Don't move, Steel Demons," a voice followed by dozens of footsteps called out from the other side of the wall. Despite the speaker not seeing me, I hardly dared to breathe. "Where's the woman you came here with?"

"Who, your wife?" the snarky reply came from Gunner. "Still passed out in my bed where I gave her the dicking of her life."

"Search inside and outside the grounds!" The speaker was not amused. "Find the biker woman and bring her to me. Then," his voice took on a cold, calculating tone, "after I'm done with her, I'll bring her to Fischlin myself."

Fuck! I couldn't stay here. I had to move. But there was literally nowhere to hide except the ravine, looking like a steep, miniature canyon as I peeked over the edge.

Taking a deep breath, I lowered myself to the edge

and slowly placed one foot on the rocky outcropping to begin my climb down.

Huge mistake.

The rock came loose and my foot slipped.

I could only grab desperate handfuls of dirt and sand as I tumbled down into painful darkness.

TWENTY

MARIPOSA

"**O**w...fuck."

Everything hurt except for my head, which was the first thing I thought of. The last thing I needed now was a concussion.

My palms, forearms, and legs, however, were a different story. I slid down some sharp rocks down into the ravine and fell about another six feet to the even rockier bottom. In a bikini, no less.

I tried to stay calm as I mentally checked myself over from head to toe, carefully wiggling fingers and other small joints before moving onto the big stuff. When it felt like nothing was broken, I let out a huge sigh of relief. The pain was intense but it all felt like bad scrapes and bruises.

"Find her! Search the ravine!"

I sprang into action, rolling to the wall of the small canyon I fell in and pressing myself against the rocks. The sky looked like a narrow tear at least ten feet above me. My heart crashed against my ribs like a drum as I waited for faces to poke into view.

Footsteps along the edge caused small showers of rocks and dust to fall on me. Fighting the urge to cough, I raised a bloodied hand to shield my eyes and mouth. The outpost guards kept walking back and forth, talking to each other in low voices.

"Fuck you, I'm not going down there!" someone cried out.

I looked around desperately, my eyes finally adjusting to the dim light. On the opposite wall was an outcropping of rocks just high enough off the ground for me to hide under. Looking up, I nearly bit a hole through my lips. If they looked while I ran to the other side, I was fucked.

"Don't be a pussy, just..."

I made a break for it, crossing to the other side in five big steps and curling into a ball under the rock shielding me from above.

"Did you hear that?"

"Just a fucking ground squirrel. Look, she can't hide forever. Me and Sen will patrol the ravine. The rest of you check the outpost perimeter. She can't have gone far..."

Their voices and footfalls eventually faded away. Still I waited, barely daring to breathe.

When my legs fell asleep from being tucked under me for so long, I dared to sit on the ground and stretch them out. After a few more minutes passed, I stole a peek at the thin sliver of sky up above me. No faces looked back at me.

Fucking now what?

They had to be at least walking along the edge of the gorge in both directions. I'd probably be safest if I stayed put. But what the hell was happening to the guys? Would they be killed? The explosion meant someone must have died or was badly injured.

Reaper!

A gasp of realization escaped me before I clapped my hand over my mouth. The SDMC president was alone. He was the most valuable person of the club, surely they wouldn't kill him. Maybe the explosion was a distraction?

A cold horror came over me, bringing goosebumps to my skin. I crossed my arms and rubbed them as I paced, trying to figure this all out.

The Steel Demons came here in good faith, I knew that for a fact. They were trying to work out an honest arrangement like what they had in Old Phoenix. I didn't know all the details of their plans, just snippets that I overheard, but I never once heard any of them trying to double-cross anyone.

They weren't the bad ones here. The owner of this place had to be in someone else's pocket. Someone trying to bring the Steel Demons down.

I was so absorbed in making sense of this mess in my head, I didn't realize that I stopped pacing and started walking.

Stopping in my tracks, another shiver came over me. But not from fear this time.

Tiny trickles of ice-cold water flowed through my sandals. I knelt down and washed off a bit of the coagulated blood and dirt off my feet. Water down here was a good sign, especially if I had to hide out for several days.

I looked back to see how far I walked. About a hundred feet, give or take. The rational part of me knew staying in one place made the most sense. But once my feet started moving, something else in me didn't want to stop.

It felt like an invisible string from my chest pulled me to keep walking through the ravine. Every instinct in me screamed to follow it, to keep going. If the feeling had a voice, it would be saying, *Someone needs you.*

I remembered this feeling. This was exactly how I felt right before checking on Kitty that last night at the service center. I chalked it up to being concerned about her, knowing about her cyst, but now without the distractions of kitchen duties, I knew it was this exact tugging sensation in my chest.

I froze for a moment, torn. For all I knew, it could have been pulling me to one of the guards looking for me. One of them might have tumbled down and sprained an ankle. Jandro and Gunner were adamant that I couldn't get caught, no matter what. Even an injured guard would likely sell me out to his boss.

But that pull was so strong. And the thought of someone injured who needed my help only made it stronger. I nearly had to brace myself against the rocky wall to keep from moving forward.

Fuck it.

I followed the trickling water, the pull immediately lessening as I placed my feet in front of each other. With one hand on the wall I kept moving, kept following my instinct.

I'd been a medic for three years and never felt this instinctual pull before. But finding whoever needed me outweighed the weirdness of this new sensation. I'd deal with it later, after getting the hell out of here and finding the guys.

The trickle of water eventually widened into a small stream running through the center of the canyon. It was still gentle and shallow, but sprang hope for a larger source of water up ahead.

I stayed glued to the wall as I continued on, not wanting to splash or give anyone above a chance to spot me. The stream gradually spread out into multiple trickles nearly the entire width of the ravine when I spotted it.

Among all the sharp-edged rocks, it was impossible to miss the softer, human form that held onto what looked like a large, black garbage bag. As I grew closer, the bag squirmed and let out a high-pitched whine.

"Oh my God!"

I broke into a run, immediately recognizing Hades squirming in the arms of Reaper.

"Mariposa?" Reaper's voice was harsher and raspier than usual. "The fuck are you doing down here?"

"I could ask you the same thing." I knelt by where he sat, leaning against a boulder with the whimpering dog squirming in his lap. "What happened?"

"He saved my life."

Reaper's voice cracked. Whether from dryness or

emotion, I couldn't tell. But hearing the stoic president as anything but stoic shocked me.

"He pulled me out of the path of the explosion right before it went off. The blast still sent us rolling down the hillside into this ravine. I tried to shield him, but he's hurt bad." Reaper's hand shot out, wrapping around my upper arm with an iron grip. His eyes glittered like two green gemstones in the darkness. "You have to help him. Please."

The coldness in him was gone. His hold on my arm was strong but had a tremor to it. And his other hand held the injured Doberman cradled like a baby against his chest. He had no overblown ego now, no pride. Whatever was between me and him didn't matter. He was just a man desperate to save his friend.

"Please, Mariposa," he repeated. "Please save him."

"Let me see him," I agreed with a nod.

Reaper released me and allowed me to come closer, loosening his hold on Hades so I could examine him.

"Shh, it's all right," he whispered, stroking the dog's muzzle. "You're gonna be okay, boy."

"He's bleeding pretty badly," I reported, my fingers moving gently over the dog's blood-soaked flank. When I applied pressure, Hades cried out in pain and kicked out to get away from me.

"Shh shh shh," Reaper wrapped his arms around his neck and closed a hand over his muzzle. "I know it hurts, boy, but you have to be quiet."

"He might have something stuck, like a piece of shrapnel," I said. "But if I try to remove it, there's a chance he could bleed out. I just can't fucking see down here."

"Let's move him into the light," Reaper nodded at the centermost trickling stream of water, directly under the sliver of sky above the canyon.

I hesitated. "But then there's a chance they'll see us."

"We've been down here for hours and no one's come searching. They must think I'm dead. Now help me move him."

"They know I'm missing," I protested. "They're looking all over for me—"

"No offense, Mari, but when it comes down to you and my dog, I'm picking my fucking dog every day of the week. Now, can you help him in better light or not?"

"Yes," I sighed, ignoring the sting of his words. "I got his legs. You hold his front half."

Taking care to move his position as little as possible, we gingerly lifted him up and side-stepped to the center. I almost forgot how muscular Hades was for a dog, and felt like I was lifting a pile of cinderblocks.

When we set him down again, the direct sunlight on his wound made a world of difference.

"Oh yeah," I confirmed. "He's got something in there."

"Can you remove it?"

"Be quiet for a second and let me check his pulse." Even right then, it felt good telling Reaper off for once. I was in my element.

"I can take it out," I decided after some careful prodding of the wound. "But I need your shirt to slow the bleeding."

Reaper set Hades' head gently on his thighs and peeled off his cut and shirt with zero argument. I jerked my eyes back down to the injured pup to concentrate.

"I can only do so much down here," I warned him. "The wound still needs to be sterilized and closed up. If we don't get out of here soon, he could bleed out or succumb to an infection."

"Do everything you can then," Reaper instructed. "And I'll worry about getting us out."

In the direct sunlight, I noticed blood trickling down his temple for the first time. It also seemed to be matted in his hair.

Without thinking, I reached for him. "You're bleeding, too—"

"Don't worry about me," he waved me off.

"Reaper, a head injury is serious—"

"I'm fine!" he snarled. "Just don't let my dog die." His voice echoed off the rocky walls and then his face softened. "Please," he added in a whisper.

I nodded, returning my attention to Hades. "It's going to hurt and he's going to struggle. I need you to hold him down."

Reaper placed his hands down on Hades' sides where I instructed, then leaned over to comfort his scared friend.

"I got you, boy," he murmured, placing kisses on the dog's forehead. Hades' tongue darted out to lick his master in response.

With my patient distracted, I reached into the open wound with my bare hand, grabbed the edge of shrapnel that I felt earlier, and pulled.

A stream of blood and Hades' panicked kicking and howling followed. I placed Reaper's shirt over the would and pressed down.

"Shh, shh," Reaper closed his muzzle again, resting his forehead on Hades. "I'm sorry, boy. I'm so sorry."

The bleeding thankfully slowed after a few minutes. I tore Reaper's shirt in half then wrapped it tightly over Hades' thigh and tied it off.

"He's stable for now," I sighed exhaustedly. "But he needs actual medical treatment within a few hours. The sooner the better."

"He's not crying anymore." Reaper almost seemed to forget I was there. His eyes were glued to his dog's face in his lap.

"He's in shock," I explained. "The body does that for pain management sometimes, but he might not respond to you."

When Reaper looked up, it felt like he was seeing me for the first time since we met in this ravine.

"Thank you."

"You're welcome." I began washing the blood off my hands in the water.

"I mean it." He gently slid Hades' head off his lap and joined me in the water. "Not everyone understands it but he's my best friend. If I lost him, I—"

My fingers drifted to the dried blood at his temple. "Will you let me check your head now?"

He smirked and splashed his face with water. "I suppose."

While checking his head and neck for any bumps or swelling, I ran my fingers through his rich brown hair more than I cared to admit. He washed his face and hands in the water and I felt like a pervert watching it stream down his naked chest and back.

"You're cold," he murmured, running a hand up my arm.

"Hmm?"

"You're covered in gooseflesh." He looked up. The sun was no longer directly over us and the sliver of bright light had all but faded. "The temperature's dropping fast."

He was right, and the freezing cold water didn't help. Except for where his hand still rested on the back of my arm, I was shivering. I wanted to lean into that touch, to lean into *him* like a cozy blanket.

"Your head seems okay," I mumbled distractedly. "Just a few bumps."

"Great," he scoffed. "So I have the same winning personality for you to deal with."

"W-why..." My teeth chattered as I hugged myself, shaking like a leaf. "Why is it suddenly so cold down here?"

"You're barely wearing any clothes, for one thing," his eyes flickered over my bikini. "And the sun never fully touches everything inside these little canyons like it does the surface. So when night falls and it cools down, it gets way colder down here."

"Is it night already?"

"Getting there. Probably close to dusk now." His hand slid from my arm down to my fingers. "Come here."

"What?"

"Just come here." One tug on my hand sent me careening into his chest. His *naked* chest. Pressing against my *nearly* naked chest.

My heart pounded like crazy and I hated that he most likely felt it. I felt his own heartbeat, calm and steady as he wrapped both arms around my back, rubbing warmth into me from his rough palms.

"I can't be having you save Hades and then let you go by freezing to death," he mumbled into my hair. "Just relax. We'll all make it out of here."

I relented, letting my head drop to his shoulder. He was a warm, solid wall as my body slumped against him. His arms felt like a blanket around me—not only warm but secure. Solid. As if nothing in the world could reach me in this protected space.

Hades whined near our feet and Reaper moved to sit next to him, pulling me down with him. Our bodies never lost contact, not even when he extended one hand to pet his dog. He even seemed to hold me tighter with the other.

I sat between his legs, my knees curled up to my chest. At some point both of Reaper's hands returned to me, moving in gentle exploration up and down my back, running through my hair.

Neither of us spoke for the longest time as the cave grew darker and colder, except to murmur some words of comfort to Hades.

Eventually, I couldn't keep it in anymore.

"I'm sorry."

Reaper's chin grazed across the top of my head. "You're sorry for what?"

"For thinking the worst of you with no proof." My lips skimmed across his chest as I spoke. "For assuming you did those things to Gretchen based on...the life you lead."

He didn't answer and his hands stopped moving. I was afraid to look up, and hardly dared to breathe. Did I say something to piss him off again?

"You made the assumption most people would have," he said softly. "But now I'm sure you know things aren't always what they seem from an outside view."

"Yes," I agreed, tentatively resting a hand on his bicep. "And I know you're not most people."

SHADOW

My brothers were in trouble.

And my president captured, or worse, dead.

But before I could find out for sure, I had to hack my way through these guardsmen tearing through every room in the outpost.

I stayed back in my room while everyone else went to the pool. Sitting out in bright sun and removing my clothing were not among my favorite things to do. Reaper had confided his unease about the deal to me last night, so I told him I'd do what I did best.

Be forgotten. Blend into the shadows. Watch and wait.

When I felt the rumble of the explosion on the other side of the building, I readied myself.

Fischlin's men were loud, their footsteps amateurish as they stormed the hallways. I squeezed the handle of my dagger in annoyance. Archers were supposed to be quiet.

"Find the woman! I want every inch of this place searched until she's found!" bellowed their leader just on the other side of the wall.

Another thing I didn't understand. Why other men were so obsessed with women. Yes, they were nice to look at and fucking them felt good, but I would be just as content to never see another one again.

My bedroom door burst open, concealing where I stood directly behind it. A man with a bow and quiver of arrows on his back began rummaging through my things, pulling back my sheets and kicking my saddle-bags. He paused and looked inside my bags with interest at the clinking of my glass liquor bottles.

Oblivious to the movement behind him, he pulled one bottle out to examine. His next breath was a gurgled choke on his blood as I slit his throat.

I wiped my knife on my cut, sheathed it, took his quiver and bow for myself, then left the room as silently as a cat.

The hallway was clear both ways, so I headed toward the direction of the explosion. A cracked open door up ahead prompted me to nock an arrow. Another guardsman was tearing that room apart, by the sound of it. I pulled back on the bowstring and loosed the arrow through the crack.

A satisfied grunt escaped me when I went to check and retrieve my arrow. I got him right in the throat. Bows weren't my favorite weapons by far, but I was decent with them. Gunner and I had a successful bowhunting trip a few years ago where he taught me how to hone in my aim. I had been so resistant to trusting him, but Jandro practically forced me to go. And I was glad I did.

Running footfalls on the tiled hallway pulled me out of nostalgia and had me spinning back to the door.

"What the aughh—"

He caught my knife with his throat as my weapon sailed the short distance between us. He fell to his knees and died before he realized what had happened, let alone remembered to alert anyone else.

I continued moving silently through the hallway, picking off any guardsmen who stood in my way. The few who saw me before they died registered me with shock and surprise in their eyes. Of course, they had forgotten all about me.

I was a big fucker, but I was silent and trailed behind the pack. Whenever I was with the group, people often ignored me. They preferred talking to Reaper or Jandro, and rightly so. I was not known for my stimulating conversation.

Only *she* attempted to speak with me, the woman all my brothers got themselves caught for. She didn't forget me and I couldn't begin to understand why. She said she liked it when I looked at her. I didn't understand that either.

It didn't matter. She would forget me eventually.

Eliminating the search party was child's play. When I reached a set of heavy, carved wooden doors guarded by four men, I knew it would be more of a challenge.

"Stop! Who are you?" their captain demanded as all four of them nocked arrows.

Saying nothing, I walked forward slowly with my

hands raised and made a big show of dropping my bow to the floor.

"He's one of them!" one of the guards declared. "The Steel Demons! He has their patch."

"Smart of you to surrender to us," their leader sneered. "Tell us where your president is and you'll be a very smart man indeed."

I kept my mouth shut but mentality filed away that Reaper hadn't been captured after all. He had to be alive, in that case.

"No?" the archer captain's lip curled as he stared at me. "We'll get you talking soon enough. Search him."

His men shouldered their bows as they approached me—empty handed and too close for shooting range. Just how I wanted them.

The moment they came close enough, my hands snapped to my back where I had two more hidden daggers sheathed. In the blink of an eye, my arms extended out to my sides with the blades firmly embedded into their chests.

"Shoot him! He's armed!"

The captain had no one left to call out to as I withdrew my blades from his two men, spun and quickly slit the throat of his third trying to ambush me from behind.

How foolish of him to think he could sneak up on a shadow.

But turning my back and dealing with him gave the captain time to react. I felt the sudden pressure of something embedded into the back of my leg. An arrow.

I barely looked at him, but didn't need to. As he reloaded, I sent a knife flying at his chest.

He stared at it, frowning as if it puzzled him for a moment before falling to his knees and face-planting dead onto the ground.

I turned him over to retrieve my blade, wiped it down, and proceeded to the set of the doors they'd been guarding.

"Shadow! Holy fuck, am I glad to see you."

The declaration came from Jandro the moment I pulled the doors open. He stood in the center of the room in a barred cage, barely tall enough for him to stand at full height or turn around in. The other members of the crew were placed in similar cages spaced throughout the room as if they were a collection of pets. For bigger, taller men like Gunner and Big G, the cells looked especially uncomfortable.

"What took you so long, big guy?" Jandro grinned as I approached.

"I had to kill everyone in my way." I examined the lock holding his cell closed.

"Figures," Gunner muttered. "The captain of those guards should have keys—"

CLANG! CLANG! CLANG!

A few hits from the handle of my dagger had Jandro's lock broken in seconds.

"All right. Thanks, King Kong," the vice president laughed as he walked out. "You smash locks, I'll grab keys and look out for anyone else."

"They don't have Reaper," I said as I moved on to Big G's cage. "They're looking for him and the woman."

"She has a name, Shadow." Gunner called from across the room. "It's Mariposa."

I shrugged before getting to work on Big G's lock. It didn't matter to me if she had a name or not.

"Holy shit, dude! You're bleeding bad." Big G's brow narrowed in concern at the arrow in my leg, which I'd forgotten all about.

"It'll stop." I reached down and snapped the shaft in half before yanking it out, which only prompted more blood to dribble onto the floor.

"Jesus fuck," Big G's face paled. "I dunno how you can do that without flinching."

I tossed the broken arrow pieces, unsure how to respond. I didn't feel pain. I hadn't felt anything remotely painful in years.

"Listen up, Demons!" Jandro raised a fist in the air once everyone was freed. "We have two priorities now— one, finding Reaper and Mariposa. Two, finding Fischlin and questioning him. Do *not* kill him, that's an order." He looked pointedly at me. "We need to question him and find out whose pocket he's really in. Anyone else we run into, feel free to kill them."

The men let out a collective cry of victory while shooting their fists in the air.

"Let's head to the armory," Gunner practically skipped out the door. "They must have stashed all of our shit there, plus extra toys that'll be fun to play with."

My brothers followed his lead while I retreated to my usual station at the back. Jandro stayed with me, looking at me with an expression I couldn't read. Not that I knew how to read many expressions.

"You all right, man?" He practically stood on tiptoes to clap me on the shoulder.

"Yes. Reaching you was easy."

"Good. Just making sure." He clapped my shoulder two more times. "You seriously saved our asses, you know. We overheard them talking about publicly executing us. I'll make sure Reaper knows what you've done."

"I didn't do it for recognition or reward. Aiding my brothers is my duty."

"I know, big guy, but still," he began jogging ahead of me to catch up with the others, "you're valuable and you shouldn't forget that."

I knew exactly what my value was—covering the others' weak spots. Aside from that, no one had any use for me. I didn't feel one way or another about that. I fully accepted my role and felt no need for anything else.

The men excitedly emptied the armory, with Gunner complaining over and over how he should have hitched an extra compartment onto his bike to bring everything home.

"Grab everything you can carry!" he instructed, stacking cases of ammo outside the door. "This'll be a much sweeter payout than our first so-called deal."

"Will you hurry the fuck up? We need to be searching, not looting," Jandro growled. "Reaper can handle himself but if they caught Mari—"

"Someone's coming." I spotted the first flicker of a shadow at the end of the corridor and drew a knife.

Six other men pointed weapons toward the guard, his face pale and his empty hands raised as he approached us.

"Don't shoot, please! I surrender!" He fell to his

knees. "I'll cooperate. I'll tell you anything you want, just let me live."

"You're full of shit," Gunner spat, shooting off one round that went wild. It hit a column and sent the man's arms wrapping around his head.

"I'm not, I swear!"

"Where's our president and our medic?" Jandro demanded.

"I don't know, we never found them! But Fischlin," he raised a hand, palm up. "He's in his office right now, gathering up valuables and documents. He's about to ride off with someone, I don't know who. But if you hurry, you might stop him!"

A beat of silence passed before Jandro sprang into action. "Big G, you stay with him. But don't kill him yet. Everyone else with me!"

He broke into a sprint, dashing down the corridor with the rest of us trailing after him. Night had fallen and the only lights were torches mounted to the columns, making it feel like were in some ancient dungeon. My chest tightened in a way that had nothing to do with my running. My scar felt hot and I could almost feel liquid dripping down the side of my face.

I knew more about dungeons than I cared to admit.

"Whoa, holy shit!"

Jandro skidded to a stop right in front of a pile of debris in our path. To our left, a massive hole in the wall looked like it wasn't supposed to be there. To the right, a dark smear on the tile floor trailed off into the wild brush of the landscape.

"This had to be the explosion!" Jandro cried. "You

guys, follow that blood trail and find our fucking president. Gunner and Shadow, with me."

"Horus is helping you guys," Gunner nodded at his men. "He'll lead you to where they are."

Jandro once tried to drunkenly explain the type of bond Gunner and Reaper had with their animals, but I couldn't easily follow. Aside from what he and Reaper did for me, I never had any kind of bond with anyone.

The three of us ran up to Fischlin's office doors a few seconds later. Jandro and Gunner both slammed their shoulders into the doors and bounced off like tennis balls.

"Move," I said.

They got out of the way just in time for my foot to crash through the heavy wood.

Gunner shook his head. "Fuck, I forget about how freakishly strong you are sometimes."

The doors were barricaded on the other side, but a few more kicks made a hole big enough for my arm to fit through. I reached through and pushed away the chairs and tables set up against the door so we could get through.

In seconds, we did.

To an empty office.

"Fucking shit!" Jandro ran to the open window, Gunner and I right on his heels.

In the distance, a motorcycle sped away, carrying two riders. My two brothers lifted their guns and started firing without another word. Behind them and over their heads, I fired off arrows from my bow, but they were already out of shooting range. The riders leaned down low from the onslaught of bullets and the driver accelerated as hard as the bike would go.

The person in the bitch seat was definitely the owner, dressed in the same loose, light-colored garb as the others who worked this outpost. The driver wore a leather cut, but it was impossible to see the patch on his back with the owner clinging to him.

"Fuck!" Jandro punched the windowsill when the riders became a mere speck on the horizon.

"We'll get 'em, bro," Gunner shouldered his weapon, looking determinedly out the window. "Maybe that prick Big G is babysitting can tell us something."

"Jandro! Captain Gunner!" One of Gunner's men came running into the office.

A screech followed him, and he ducked just in time to avoid getting clawed by Horus swooping in to land on his master's shoulder.

"Please tell me something good," Jandro sighed.

Gunner's man beamed with pride. "We found all of them, sir. Reaper, the medic, and Hades. They're stuck in a ravine and we need a rope."

It didn't take much looking to find a thick, nautical rope to drop into the ravine. Looking over the edge, I saw the woman huddled up against Reaper, shivering and barely wearing anything. Hades laid next to them, a crude bloodsoaked bandage wrapped around his rear leg.

"Fuckin' pitch black down there," one of Gunner's men mumbled as he came over with a torch.

"I can see them," I said but he tossed the torch down

anyway. It bounced with a hiss over the streams of trickling water running through the cave.

"Tryin' to get us killed down here?" Reaper bellowed from down below.

"No, President," I called back. "The others can't see you that well."

"Shadow! I've never been so happy to see your ugly mug. Pull her up first."

I felt a slight weight on my rope a few seconds later and started hauling it up. The woman was covered in dirt and dried blood. Her arms and legs wrapped tightly around the rope like her life depended on it.

"Mariposa!" Jandro called from behind me, his footsteps approaching quickly.

"Baby girl!" Gunner called. "Are you all right?"

When I finished pulling her up to solid ground, I expected her to run straight to them. Women always ran to the handsome men. But to my surprise and confusion, it was *my* neck she wrapped arms around. Her feet dangled above the ground as she clung to me tightly.

"Thank you for saving us," she whispered in my ear.

MARIPOSA

H ades' large, dilated eyes followed me as I cleaned up my supplies. His tongue hung out the corner of his mouth, which further softened his intimidating appearance. A patch of shaved fur showed off the jagged incision on his flank held together by my sutures.

"That's my boy," Reaper laid on the floor next to him, just outside of the pile of pillows serving as a temporary dog bed. "High as a kite," he chuckled, stroking down Hades' side.

"He won't need another dose for about twelve hours," I rolled my gloves off and shoved them into my trash bag. "He might be lethargic from all the meds for a day or two."

"Oh, we won't be going anywhere right away," Reaper's eyes flashed as he sat up. "We're tearing this place apart for information and living like kings while we're at it."

"Have they interviewed that guard yet?"

"No, but he's being sat on twenty-four seven. I'll talk to him after he's had some time to sweat."

The Steel Demons' president watched me silently as I sterilized my tools and laid them out on a side table. "Why didn't you heal Shadow's arrow wound?" he asked.

"Because he walked away from me when I offered," I asked. "Which I took to mean he was refusing my help."

"Why didn't you do it anyway? I thought healing was the most important thing to you."

"It is," I breathed. "But I can't treat someone against their will. I need their consent. Especially now."

"Why's that?"

"Because in a world like this," I spread my hands around. "With no laws or rights to protect us, our bodies are the last thing we have control over. To treat someone when they've said no is violating that final piece of personal control, even if it's to their benefit."

Reaper's eyes rolled back to his dog laid out on the floor. "What about animals? Hades can't tell you yes or no. He probably didn't understand down in that ravine and thought you were hurting him."

"I just have to make my best guess," I shrugged. "He saved you, so I imagine he wanted to keep on living to protect you and stay by your side. And something tells me," I paused, "Hades is more intelligent than your average dog."

"What if," Reaper rose from the floor, coming toward me with a slow swagger, "I *ordered* you to treat my men, no matter what they said? If I had Jandro or

Gunner strapped down because of some ailment and they were screaming at you to get away, would you treat them if I ordered it?"

I squared my shoulders toward him, refusing to be intimidated. He was using his president's voice and sharp gaze, but I had seen the softness in him. I heard in his voice how worried he was about losing Hades. He held me against that beating heart in his broad chest so I wouldn't freeze to death. Who knew if his men ever saw that side of him, but I'd never forget it.

"No one has that kind of power," I told him. "Not even you."

"Not even if I punish you?" A wicked smile came to his lips. "Humiliate you with a public lashing, maybe?"

"You can deal out whatever barbaric punishment suits you," I answered. "That doesn't change the fact that you ordered me to violate your men's rights to govern their own bodies. How much would they respect and obey you if you denied them this? If they survived this hypothetical ailment, they'd know you see them as nothing more than slaves."

"Some would say it's better off that way," he responded coolly, his eyes searching mine. "They're rounding up people like cattle in the Southern territories."

"That's not you," I said with a shake of my head. "You're better than that."

"How do you know?" he snapped.

"Because you treat your dog like a family member," I said. "The respect between you and your men is mutual. And you have..."

"What?" he demanded, leaning forward so his face was an inch from mine. His hands braced on the table on either side of me, caging me in. "What do I have that a slave owner doesn't?"

"You have a moral code." His lips and the dark stubble surrounding them consumed my vision. "You value honesty and trust. And you," my eyes lifted to his, "you don't hurt those weaker than you."

Reaper pulled back for a moment, turning his gaze to the window. "Fucking hell. I knew this shit would happen."

I blinked. "What?"

He turned back to me, and the next thing I felt was the heat of his mouth on mine.

My lips parted in shock and his tongue wasted no time in pressing between them, the weight of his hands now on my lower back and pulling me forward. Just like the first time, each kiss was effortless, seamless.

He'd been so calm and detached down in that cave with a steady heartbeat. Now it raced under my palm through the thin shirt he wore. I groped down his chest, feeling for the hem of his shirt to remove the barrier between his skin and mine. I *needed* that heat again, to feel the texture of his scars and the coarse hair dusting his chest and under his navel.

He pawed at my top with the same frenzy, his hands roaming further than they ever did in that ravine. When my flimsy bra came off, his mouth fell to my neck as his hands swept forward to my chest.

At the first sensation of his calloused hands on my breasts, my head dipped back with a shameless moan.

My whole body responded with a shiver at his rough thumbpads pressing over my nipples.

"Sensitive here, huh?" he murmured at the base of my throat before his lips trailed down my skin to meet his hands.

"Yeah." The word came out a breathy whisper as I braced one hand on the table behind me. A dull ache pulsed between my legs, growing needier with every caress and swipe of Reaper's tongue.

I grabbed the sides of his face, returning his mouth to mine with a fierce hunger. An amused chuckle rumbled through him. I felt it from my lips all the way to my core, stretching on my tiptoes to kiss him harder, to taste him deeper.

His hands slid down to my ass, grabbing each side with a firm hold that bordered on painful. That small hint of roughness sent me climbing him like a tree, gluing my inner thighs to his hips until my feet left the ground and locked behind him. He helped me up, holding me securely by my ass as he lifted me off the table and turned toward the bedroom of his fancy suite.

Thump-thump-thump-thump!

A knock startled me mid-kiss and Reaper let out an annoyed growl.

"Not now!" he yelled at the door.

"Sir," it sounded like one of Gunner's men. "The VP and Captain Gunner want to meet with you about—"

"I fucking said *not now*! One more word gets you a black eye, kid!"

His next kiss was rougher—full of teeth, possessiveness, and growling groans. I grew lightheaded with desire at the sudden change, molding my body to his as I returned his kisses with equal passion. I wanted, no, *needed* to hear those moans from him again. When he laid me down on his unmade bed with surprising gentleness, I came to the stark realization I wasn't afraid of him anymore.

"What if that was important?" I asked, looking up at him.

"Even if it is, it can wait." His fingers slid into the waistband of my scrub pants, yanking them down my legs. "Nothing is as important as this right now," he smoothed a hand up my thigh, rough fingertips tracing over my hip bones.

"Oh, really?" I tried to make my tone flirty but I had to know something before *this* happened. "Does that mean you won't ignore me anymore after you get off?"

He didn't answer but laid on his side next to me. Silently, he traced small circles on my hips and lower belly.

His silence made me so insecure, I couldn't stop myself from rambling. "I'm not asking for this to be any more than sex. I'm fine with that, just, you know. Can we put everything else behind us?"

His hand slid across my ribcage, cupping my breast before his palm met the mattress on the other side of me. Then he was on top of me, green eyes practically glowing.

"You saved my dog, my best friend," he said. "I can't put into words how important that makes you."

His mouth descended on mine again with the same passion as before, but full of tenderness rather than rough bites. There were so many layers to this man and I had a feeling I'd barely scratched the surface.

As his thighs nudged mine apart, I slid my palm down the horned skull inked on his chest. After rows of hard abs, my hand met an equally hard bulge straining to be freed from his jeans.

His moan through his kiss was so loud and hot. I loved that I could feel him as well as hear him.

He helped me unbutton and unzip him with a hurried hand, allowing me to shove his pants down muscular thighs that clearly knew how to ride both a motorcycle and a woman.

His lower half, cock included, was just as tanned as the sunkissed olive glow of his upper body. A surge of heat and desire ran through me at the thought of this glorious naked man lying out in the sun. He graced me with another sexy moan, this time vibrating against my neck, as my hand wrapped around the base of his thick shaft.

"Yes," he hissed in a tight whisper as I stroked upward, following the curve of his luscious cock. "Just like that."

Cradling my head in one hand, his fist tightened in my hair as he pulled. Staring at the headboard, the column of my throat exposed, he alternated between rough and gentle kisses on the sensitive flesh of my neck. I felt his hips move, beginning to thrust into my hand as he nipped my throat.

His other hand made a slow, lazy descent down my body, stopping for detours at my breasts, my waist, and both hip bones before venturing between my legs. He let out a pleased hum at what he found here.

"I take it you're enjoying yourself?" he murmured, slicking his fingers in slow, teasing exploration of my sex.

"Mmm," was all I could reply, writhing wantonly against his hand.

I enjoyed what he was doing most of all, but words and sentences escaped me. From head to toe, I was nothing but a body filled with the most basic, primal need.

"Getting eager, are we?" Reaper smirked as my hips lifted off the mattress, one leg clinging to his side with my foot pressing into his calf.

"I didn't think you brought me to bed just so we could get to third base." I released his shaft and cupped his balls, tugging slightly as I watched his face.

"Fuck," he hissed and went rigid, pulling away for a moment to stare at the blank wall.

"Enjoying yourself, I take it?" I teased, raking my nails lightly down his thighs. "Maybe a little too much?"

He barked out a laugh, holding my jaw as he brushed his thumb across my lip.

"I should've known an educated woman came with a smart mouth," his lips hovered above mine. "I broke a personal commandment bringing you into my club, now I'm bringing you into my bed. What have you done to me, Mariposa?"

Rhetorical question or not, I had no chance to answer. He lowered himself down, aligned his silky, round head to my sex and pressed forward.

I cried out, more from surprise than pain, my moan

quickly swallowed by a deep kiss as Reaper began moving.

Holy...fuck, was all I could think as he entered and left me. That upward curve hit all the right spots and then some. I held onto his wide, muscular back like I might come apart at any moment.

"Fuck," he groaned again, pausing his thrusts while fully sheathed inside me. His breaths came in ragged pants as he kissed and nipped every part of me that his mouth could reach.

"Something wrong?" I asked, my own pants matching his.

"No, sugar. Not at all." He tenderly brushed a piece of hair off my face. "I just want to feel you for a minute."

His cock pulsed inside me, filling up the aching emptiness that never felt so torturous until I met him and his men. *Wait...probably shouldn't be thinking about the other guys right now. Just focus on him. It's not like he isn't hot enough.*

I spent the pause in his movement doing just the same—feeling him. I ran my fingers through his dark brown hair that started growing longer. My fingertips traveled over his neck, his shoulders and biceps, pausing on the pale scars that dotted his olive skin. I traced the veins in his forearms, taking them in like winding blue rivers. When I moved to his chest, outlining the grinning, horned skull, he brought another kiss down on me. His hips rolled, abs flexing as he moved that dick inside me again.

I held onto him tighter, digging my nails into his

back as my hips lifted. My clit tingled with increasing intensity as I matched him thrust for thrust.

"Don't stop this time," I whispered desperately in his ear.

The growling moan he answered with was the hottest sound I ever heard any man make.

He crashed into me faster, pressing me down into the bed with the impact of each thrust. My own moans became desperate whimpers as my orgasm peaked higher and higher, nearing its tipping point but always just out of reach.

"Mariposa," Reaper groaned into my neck, his fists tightening into my hair.

His cock swelled inside me just as my release convulsed around him. Hearing him moan my name was like the key that unlocked my pleasure. His warmth spilled inside me, shivers wracking his whole body as my pussy milked him.

We stayed locked together until we both came down from our highs. With post-orgasm clarity, I half expected him to roll over and fall asleep. Worst case, he'd shoo me off to my own room.

Instead he pulled me with him as he rolled onto his back, holding me against his chest with his arms around my waist. After a few moments, I heard his deep breathing with his lips on my hair.

REAPER

Mariposa rolled away from me at some point while we slept. I also woke up to find Hades sleeping at the foot of the bed, but that wasn't entirely unexpected. He never left my side while in perfect health. His instincts didn't change even while drugged up and injured.

I rolled to my side, scooting closer to Mariposa's back. Not caring if I woke her, I nestled my palm into her waist and dragged my lips against the nape of her neck.

I loved how her curves fit against me, how responsive and sensitive she was. My cock twitched from where it pressed against her ass. If Hades wasn't in bed with us like a stage-5 clinger, I wouldn't have hesitated to go another round with her.

"Hmm."

Mariposa moaned sweetly as she stretched, her toes and fingers curling as she rolled over to face me.

"You're still here," she murmured sleepily, as if surprised by that.

I remembered her comment about this being nothing more than sex, which seemed to be in the same vein. She trusted me more than before, but still expected me to use and discard her. I wasn't sure how to tell her that wasn't where my head was.

"I don't want to go back to work yet." I traced her jaw, bringing her lips to mine for an open-mouthed kiss.

I wasn't normally such a kissy guy, but I couldn't get enough of how she tasted. Next time, I absolutely had to taste her pussy. She must have tasted divine.

"Hades," she giggled, noticing his big black form at the end of the bed. "You aren't supposed to be jumping on things, silly boy." She scratched his head with her toes, making him grunt and look at us upside down.

"Can't keep a good dog down," I mumbled against her cheek, dragging my mouth down to her collarbone. Fucking hell, her taste and smell were nothing short of intoxicating.

"So what's next?" she asked, her lips brushing my forehead.

I took my time kissing her collarbone before answering. "Next, we can fuck in the shower. Maybe by the pool. Somewhere the gimpy mutt won't follow us."

She laughed lightly, scooting down to rest her head on my shoulder. "So this is something you want to repeat?"

"Yes." I rested my hand on her waist again. "That sounds like a loaded question, though."

Her fingers began tracing the Steel Demons tattoo on my chest. "Will you be sleeping with others?"

My hand began mimicking hers, fingertips tracing on her skin. "I don't plan on it."

Her hand stopped.

"You don't plan on it," she repeated.

"If you want something from me, just come out and say it," I said. "I should warn you, though, I don't do traditional relationships."

"I know," she whispered. "Noelle told me a little about how you grew up. In the matriarchal communities."

"Yeah? What'd she tell you?"

"That you had one mother and three fathers. That it was accepted for women to be with multiple men at the same time."

"Yeah, and look how well that turned out," I scoffed. "The Collapse put an end to those communities."

"What happened to your family?" she looked up at me. "How did you end up as an MC's president?"

"A long story for another day, sugar," I stroked my fingers through her hair. "Preferably after I find out who wants my club annihilated."

She was quiet for a moment. "Then can you tell me what happened to your brother?"

I almost said no. My own story was long and bloody, but it was mine. Ultimately I didn't care who knew it. But Daren's was different, partly because he was such a different person than me. He was bright-eyed and hopeful, nowhere near as jaded as me. I wanted to keep those memories of him close to my chest, a well-guarded secret. He deserved to be remembered as how he was, not how he died.

If it were any other woman next to me, I would have told her to mind her own fucking business. But somehow, I knew Mariposa would understand.

"Daren was nothing like me and Noelle," I said. "He was the youngest of us three, but acted like a fourth father sometimes." Mari's lips curved into a smile at that. "Noelle and I were the daredevils," I went on. "We had drinking and smoking contests in our teens. We stole a tattoo gun once and gave each other our first tattoos." I raised my arm to show her the faded blue squiggle near my wrist. "And it was never our parents scolding us, it was Daren. But as the world got shittier and the Collapse became imminent, he always believed things would get better."

"I used to think the same thing," Mari answered softly, her fingers resuming tracing the lines of ink on my chest.

"Right, well," I sighed. "Long story short, the club rode through this little shanty town near the old Utah border a bit over a year ago. Hardly anything was there, so we rode through without stopping. Not even a full day later, everyone is fucking sick. Like, deathly ill."

Mari's eyes widened. "A virus? Some kind of airborne bio-weapon?"

"That's what we think," I said. "Some asshole might've bombed the place in a border war. Anyway, we were all on death's doorstep and could barely sit on our fucking bikes. Somehow, we found a small clinic and just raided the fucking place. We shot ourselves up with every vaccine we could find. We holed up there for a week and most of us started to feel better."

My hand curled into a fist in her hair. I didn't even know if I could bring myself to say what happened next. I never talked about it. Everyone was there and saw it for themselves.

"Daren didn't get better." Mari said it for me.

"We were one short on the last vaccine. I don't even remember what it was," I said. Once I started talking, it all seemed to spill out of me. "I tried to make him take it but he refused. He said I needed to beat whatever this shit was, because I was president and the club needed me. '*The world needs you. She needs you,*' he said. He was already so weak, he was just babbling nonsense. I told him I'd take half the syringe if he took the other half. He finally agreed but when he stuck me, he emptied the whole syringe into my arm."

I rubbed my forehead as though trying to wipe that memory away. "God, I was so fucking pissed at him."

"I'm sorry," Mari whispered. "But if you had split the vaccine, probably both of you would have died."

"Good. Then he wouldn't have died alone."

"But then you wouldn't have Hades," she protested. "And your men would be lost without you."

And I wouldn't have you, naked and beautiful lying next to me.

While few and far between, I had my moments where I was grateful to be alive. Despite talking about something deeply uncomfortable to me, this was one of those moments. If I had to talk about it, I was glad it was with her. And not only because she felt like heaven wrapped around my dick hours earlier. She stayed calm and comforting without going into hysterics like some women did.

Even so, talking about Daren set a dark cloud over my mood. I needed to think about anything else.

"I should go interview this guard," I said, rolling upright. I gave Hades a few pats before looking around for my clothes. "You can stay here if you want," I told Mari. "Or walk the grounds, go down to eat. It should be safe to walk around anywhere now."

"Can I go with you?" she asked, biting her lip as if bashful.

"Probably not a good idea," I mused, tucking my junk into my pants before zipping up. "Depending on how cooperative he is, we might need to get creative extracting information out of him."

"You're going to torture him?" her eyes widened.

"I'm going to do what's necessary to find out who wants us dead." I leaned over the bed, holding her chin in my hands. "This is your life now, sugar. I'm not the worst of men, but I'm still not a good one."

She said nothing, but I saw the wheels turning in her head as she stared back at me defiantly. When I lowered my mouth to hers, she kissed me back, sending a jolt of pleasure straight to my cock when she bit my lower lip and tugged.

Hmm. Maybe my sweet medic had a little bad girl in her after all.

"On second thought," I groaned, my lips still pressed

to hers, "you better be right here when I get back. Naked and wet for me."

"Hmm," she pursed her lips, a smirk tugging at one corner. "I'll think about it."

"You'll do it. If you want to come, that is."

She lifted one shoulder in a shrug. "Maybe I like a little delayed gratification."

"You don't want to test me, woman," I growled, cupping the side of her neck. "That is not a game you will win."

"You've never played with *me* before," she grinned before pressing lightly on my chest. "Go. Do your interrogation before I change my mind completely."

"You won't," I promised her, stealing one more kiss before turning to leave.

Just before reaching the door, I heard Hades grunt and whine, wishing to follow me. Then Mari's voice comforting him, no doubt giving him pets and telling him I'd be back.

It brought a smile to my face, a rare one of genuine joy. I got weirded the fuck out when he took to her so quickly. Now it almost seemed like it was meant to happen.

"That good, huh?"

Jandro stood right outside my door, arms crossed and eyes narrowed suspiciously. "I haven't seen you smile like that in a long-ass time."

"Fuck off," I snapped. "Who posted you at my door like my fucking keeper?"

"Just waiting for you to join us. But it's clear you're off doing," he licked his lips, "*much* better things."

"I do like to think I have my priorities in order. So, shall we?"

"How's the pooch?" he asked as we started walking.

"Better than expected," I admitted. "I almost thought I lost him. But Mari worked like hell to save him. He'll be on antibiotics and painkillers for a while, but right as rain in a few weeks."

"Mm-hmm. And I'm sure you thanked her properly," he said with a jab to my arm.

"I'd like to think so," I smirked. "I might a few more times just to make sure."

"Damn. Leave some for the rest of us, Reap," he laughed. The grin left his face the moment he saw my ponderous expression. "Wait, you're not actually thinking...?"

"I'm not thinking anything yet," I said dismissively. "It's too soon to tell. But she," I sucked in a breath, "she seems convinced I'll fuck anything that walks by. So if you and Gunner keep getting close to her and something happens, maybe she'll feel better about it."

"Did you actually *tell* her you don't work that way?"

"Not exactly," I sighed. "Like I said, it's too soon. For all I know, she just wants to use *me* as a fuck toy."

"You know it's not like that," Jandro shook his head. "At some point, you're gonna have to tell her sharing her with other men means she's special to you."

"I will if it gets to that," I snapped. "But she's still wrapping her mind around being in an MC. Let me fuck her a few more dozen times before we talk about getting serious."

We walked in silence down the corridor, our boots

echoing off the stone tiles. The outpost was gloriously empty and it felt amazing not having some sneaky fuckers watching us at all times.

"She's not the only one who'll have to wrap her head around it," Jandro murmured. "You know Gunner's sweet on her, but he's the poster boy for pre-Collapse America. He doesn't get the whole matriarchal sharing thing."

"We'll cross that bridge when we come to it," I said through gritted teeth.

Jandro was a strategic and thorough thinker. His intelligence was a huge asset to me, but goddamn if his habit of thinking ten steps ahead didn't grate on me sometimes.

Gunner wore a grim expression at his post as we approached the room where our prisoner was guarded.

"President," he greeted me with a curt nod. He wasn't usually so formal with me. Was he sour because I fucked Mari?

"Is he talking?" I nodded at the set of doors behind him, choosing to ignore his sourpuss mood.

"Oh yeah. He didn't hold nothing back." Gunner's frown deepened.

"And?"

"It's worse than we thought."

"Quit playing hard to get, Gun. Fucking spill it."

"He said the man paying Fischlin to capture and kill us," his hands drifted to his weapons on his belt, "was none other than General Tash."

TO BE CONTINUED IN POWERLESS - BOOK 2
OF THE STEEL DEMONS MC SERIES.

POWERLESS IS AVAILABLE NOW!
CLICK HERE TO START READING.

Also by Crystal Ash

Harem of Freaks: The Complete Series

Say Your Prayers

Steel Demons MC

Lawless

Powerless

Fearless

Painless

Helpless

Heartless

Senseless

Ruthless

Merciless

Endless

Shifted Mates Trilogy

Unholy Trinity: The Complete Series

For a complete list of books by Crystal Ash, visit her Amazon page.

About the Author

Crystal Ash is a USA Today Bestselling Author from California. She loves writing steamy, heart-wrenching romance with tortured heroes, especially if they're in a reverse harem. Crystal's other loves include animals, mythology, and well-crafted alcohol, most of which can also be found in her stories.

When she's not writing, she's probably drinking craft beer with her husband or trying to coax her feral cat into accepting affection.

crystalashbooks.com

facebook.com/Crystal.Ash.Romance

instagram.com/crystalashbooks

amazon.com/author/crystalash

bookbub.com/profile/crystal-ash